"This is the one."

The minute she put on the wedding gown, Natalie knew it. Delicate silver-stitched designs looked like snowflakes dancing across the fabric. It was the most beautiful dress she'd ever seen, and she'd seen hundreds of brides come through her chapel.

It was perfect. Everything she'd ever wanted.

Natalie swallowed hard. Everything she'd ever wanted *for the bride*, she corrected herself.

Quickly she turned to Colin. He said nothing as he walked toward her. Did he hate it?

She felt her chest tighten. He wasn't looking at the gown. He was looking at her. The intensity of his gaze made her insides turn molten. Her knees started trembling.

Just when she thought she couldn't bear his gaze any longer, she turned back around. But this time she caught his reflection in the mirror beside her. Maybe it was the confusion of playing the part of the bride...but for one moment he looked like a groom.

Her groom.

* * *

A White Wedding Christmas is part of the Brides and Belles series: Wedding planning is their business...and their pleasure

Dear Reader,

You would think that someone who organized weddings for a living would dream about having a wedding of her own one day. That's anything but true in Natalie's case. She's so jaded by the relationships she's seen fail, she refuses to take the risk herself. In a time where 40 to 50 percent of marriages end in divorce, it can seem like a lost cause. I know that I've watched several friends go through long, painful and near-devastating divorces. But I've also seen those same friends find love and hope again.

I needed to find just the right person to make Natalie take the leap, and who better than the man who made her heart flutter long before reality intruded on her dreams? Colin wants and believes in marriage and family, and it's his confidence that will make even the ever-jaded Natalie believe in love again.

If you enjoy Natalie and Colin's story, tell me by visiting my website at andrealaurence.com, like my fan page on Facebook or follow me on Twitter. I'd love to hear from you!

Enjoy,

Andrea

A WHITE WEDDING CHRISTMAS

ANDREA LAURENCE

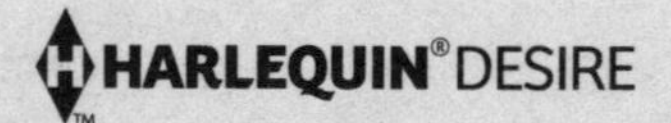

If you purchased this book without a cover you should be aware that this book is stolen property. It was reported as "unsold and destroyed" to the publisher, and neither the author nor the publisher has received any payment for this "stripped book."

Recycling programs for this product may not exist in your area.

ISBN-13: 978-0-373-73429-0

A White Wedding Christmas

Copyright © 2015 by Andrea Laurence

All rights reserved. Except for use in any review, the reproduction or utilization of this work in whole or in part in any form by any electronic, mechanical or other means, now known or hereinafter invented, including xerography, photocopying and recording, or in any information storage or retrieval system, is forbidden without the written permission of the publisher, Harlequin Enterprises Limited, 225 Duncan Mill Road, Don Mills, Ontario M3B 3K9, Canada.

This is a work of fiction. Names, characters, places and incidents are either the product of the author's imagination or are used fictitiously, and any resemblance to actual persons, living or dead, business establishments, events or locales is entirely coincidental.

This edition published by arrangement with Harlequin Books S.A.

For questions and comments about the quality of this book, please contact us at CustomerService@Harlequin.com.

® and TM are trademarks of Harlequin Enterprises Limited or its corporate affiliates. Trademarks indicated with ® are registered in the United States Patent and Trademark Office, the Canadian Intellectual Property Office and in other countries.

Printed in U.S.A.

Andrea Laurence is an award-winning author of contemporary romance for Harlequin Desire and paranormal romance for Harlequin Nocturne. She has been a lover of reading and writing stories since she learned to read at a young age. She always dreamed of seeing her work in print and is thrilled to share her special blend of sensuality and dry, sarcastic humor with the world.

A dedicated West Coast girl transplanted into the Deep South, Andrea is working on her own happily-ever-after with her boyfriend and their collection of animals, including a Siberian husky that sheds like nobody's business. If you enjoy Colin and Natalie's story, tell her by visiting her website, andrealaurence.com; like her fan page at facebook.com/authorandrealaurence; or follow her on Twitter, @andrea_laurence.

Books by Andrea Laurence

Harlequin Desire

Brides and Belles

Snowed In with Her Ex
Thirty Days to Win His Wife
One Week with the Best Man
A White Wedding Christmas

Secrets of Eden

Undeniable Demands
A Beauty Uncovered
Heir to Scandal
Her Secret Husband

Visit her Author Profile page at Harlequin.com, or andrealaurence.com, for more titles.

To Diet Coke & Jelly Belly—

A lot of people have supported me throughout my career and over the course of my multiple releases, I've done my best to thank them all. Now that I have, it would be remiss if I failed to thank the two crucial elements of my daily word count: caffeine and sugar. My preferred delivery methods are Diet Coke and Jelly Belly jelly beans (strawberry margarita, pear and coconut, to be precise). They have helped me overcome plot challenges and allowed me to keep up with my insane deadline schedule.

Prologue

A lot had changed in the past fourteen years.

Fourteen years ago, Natalie and her best friend, Lily, were inseparable, and Lily's older brother Colin was the tasty treat Natalie had craved since she was fifteen. Now, Lily was about to get married and their engagement party was being held at the large, sprawling estate of her brother.

He'd come a long way since she saw him last. She'd watched, smitten, as he'd evolved into the cool college guy, and when Lily and Colin's parents died suddenly, Natalie had watched him turn into thc rcsponsible guardian of his younger sister and the head of his father's company. He'd been more untouchable then than ever before.

Lily and Natalie hadn't seen much of each other over the past few years. Natalie had gone to college at the

University of Tennessee and Lily had drifted aimlessly. They exchanged the occasional emails and Facebook likes, but they hadn't really talked in a long time. She'd been surprised when Lily called her at From This Moment, the wedding company Natalie co-owned, with a request.

A quickie wedding. Before Christmas, if possible. It had been early November at the time, and From This Moment usually had at least fourteen months of weddings scheduled in advance. But they closed at Christmas and for a friend, she and the other three ladies that owned and operated the wedding chapel agreed to squeeze one more wedding in before the holiday.

Natalie's invitation for the engagement party arrived the next day and now, here she was, in a cocktail dress, milling around Colin's huge house filled with people she didn't know.

That wasn't entirely true. She knew the bride. And when her gaze met the golden hazel eyes she'd fantasized about as a teenager, she remembered she knew a second person at the party, too.

"Natalie?" Colin said, crossing a room full of people to see her.

It took her a moment to even find the words to respond. This wasn't the boy she remembered from her youth. He'd grown into a man with broad shoulders that filled out his expensive suit coat, a tanned complexion with eyes that crinkled as he smiled and a five-o'clock shadow that any teenager would've been proud to grow.

"It is you," he said with a grin before he moved in for a hug.

Natalie steadied herself for the familiar embrace. Not everything had changed. Colin had always been a hugger. As a smitten teen, she'd both loved and hated those hugs. There was a thrill that ran down her spine from being so close; a tingle danced across her skin as it brushed his. Now, just as she did then, she closed her eyes and breathed in the scent of him. He smelled better than he did back when he wore cheap drugstore cologne, but even then, she'd loved it.

"How are you, Colin?" she asked as they parted. Natalie hoped her cheeks weren't flushing red. They felt hot, but that could just be the wine she'd been drinking steadily since she got to the party.

"I'm great. Busy with the landscaping business, as always."

"Right." Natalie nodded. "You're still running your dad's company, aren't you?"

He nodded, a hint of suppressed sadness lighting in his eyes for just a moment. *Good going, Natalie, remind him of his dead parents straight off.*

"I'm so glad you were able to fit Lily's wedding in at your facility. She was adamant that the wedding happen there."

"It's the best," Natalie said and it was true. There was no other place like their chapel in Nashville, Tennessee, or anywhere else she knew of. They were one of a kind, providing everything a couple needed for a wedding at one location.

"Good. I want the best for Lily's big day. You look amazing, by the way. Natalie is all grown up," Colin noted.

Natalie detected a hint of appreciation in his eyes as his gaze raked over the formfitting blue dress her business partner Amelia had forced her into wearing tonight. Now she was happy her fashion-conscious friend had dressed her up for the night. She glanced at Colin's left hand—no ring. At one point, she'd heard he was married, but it must not have worked out. Shocker. That left the possibilities open for a more interesting evening than she'd first anticipated tonight.

"I'm nearly thirty now, you know. I'm not a teenager."

Colin let out a ragged breath and forced his gaze back up to her face. "Thank goodness. I'd feel like a dirty old man right now if you were."

Natalie's eyebrow went up curiously. He *was* into her. The unobtainable fantasy might actually be within her grasp. Perhaps now was the time to make the leap she'd always been too chicken to make before. "You know, I have a confession to make." She leaned into him, resting a hand on his shoulder. "I was totally infatuated with you when we were kids."

Colin grinned wide. "Were you, now?"

"Oh yes." And she wouldn't mind letting those old fantasies run wild for a night. "You know, the party is starting to wind down. Would you be interested in getting out of here and finding someplace quiet where we could talk and catch up?"

Natalie said the words casually, but her body language read anything but. She watched as Colin swallowed hard, the muscles in his throat working up and down as he considered her offer. It was bold, and she knew it, but she might not have another chance to get a taste of Colin Russell.

"I'd love to catch up, Natalie, but unfortunately I can't."

Natalie took a big sip of her wine, finishing her glass, and nodded, trying to cover the painful flinch at his rejection. Suddenly she was sixteen again and felt just as unworthy of Colin's attentions as ever. Whatever.

"Well, that's a shame. I'll see you around then," she said, shrugging it off as though it was nothing but a casual offer. Turning on her heel with a sly smile, she made her way through the crowd and fled the party before she had to face any more embarrassment.

One

Putting together a decent wedding in a month was nearly impossible, even with someone as capable as Natalie handling things. Certain things took time, like printing invitations, ordering wedding dresses, coordinating with vendors… Fortunately at From This Moment wedding chapel, she and her co-owners and friends handled most of the work.

"Thank you for squeezing this last wedding in," Natalie said as they sat around the conference room table at their Monday morning staff meeting. "I know you all would much rather be starting your holiday celebrations."

"It's fine," Bree Harper, the photographer, insisted. "Ian and I aren't leaving for Aspen until the following week."

"It gives me something to do until Julian can fly back

from Hollywood," Gretchen McAlister added. "We're driving up to Louisville to spend the holidays with his family, and working another wedding will keep me from worrying about the trip."

"You've already met his family, Gretchen. Why are you nervous?"

"Because this time I'm his fiancée," Gretchen said, looking down in amazement at the ring he'd just given to her last week.

Natalie tried not to notice that all of her formerly single friends were now paired off. Gretchen and Bree were engaged. Amelia was married and pregnant. At one time, they had all been able to commiserate about their singleness, but now, it was just Natalie who went home alone each night. And she was okay with that. She anticipated a lifetime of going home alone. It's just that the status quo had changed so quickly for them all. The past year had been a whirlwind of romance for the ladies at From This Moment.

Despite the fact that she was a wedding planner, Natalie didn't actually believe in any of that stuff. She got into the industry with her friends because they'd asked her to, for one thing. For the other, it was an amazingly lucrative business. Despite the dismal marriage statistics, people seemed happy to take the leap, shelling out thousands of dollars, only to shell out more to their divorce attorneys at some point down the road.

As far as Natalie was concerned, every couple who walked through the door was doomed. The least she could do was give them a wedding to remember. She'd do her best to orchestrate a perfect day they could look back on. It was all downhill from there, anyway.

"I'll have the digital invitations ready by tomorrow.

Do you have the list of email addresses for me to send them out?" Gretchen asked.

Natalie snapped out of her thoughts and looked down at her tablet. "Yes, I have the list here." Normally, e-invites were out of the question for a formal wedding, but there just wasn't time to get paper ones designed, printed, addressed, mailed and gather RSVPs in a month's time.

"We're doing a winter wonderland theme, you said?" Amelia asked.

"That's what Lily mentioned. She was pretty vague about the whole thing. I've got an appointment with them on the calendar for this afternoon, so we'll start firming everything up then. Bree, you're doing engagement photos on Friday morning, right?"

"Yep," Bree said. "They wanted to take their shots at the groom's motorcycle shop downtown."

Natalie had known Lily a long time, but her choice in a future husband was a surprise even to her. Frankie owned a custom motorcycle shop. He was a flannel-wearing, bushy-bearded, tattooed hipster who looked more like a biker raised by lumberjacks than a successful businessman. Definitely not who Natalie would have picked for her best friend, and she was pretty sure he was not who Colin would've picked for Lily, either.

He seemed like a nice guy, though, and even Natalie could see that under the tattoos and hair, the guy was completely hormone pair-bonded to Lily. She wouldn't say they were in love because she didn't believe in love. But they were definitely pair-bonded. Biology was a powerful thing in its drive to continue the species. They could hardly keep their hands off each other at the engagement party.

"Okay. If that's all for this morning," Bree said, "I'm going to head to the lab and finish processing Saturday's wedding photos."

Natalie looked over her checklist. "Yep, that's it."

Bree and Amelia got up, filing out of the conference room, but Gretchen loitered by the table. She watched Natalie for a moment with a curious expression on her face. "What's going on with you? You seem distracted. Grumpier than usual."

That was sweet of her to point out. She knew she wasn't that pleasant this time of year, but she didn't need her friends reminding her of it. "Nothing is going on with me."

Gretchen crossed her arms over her chest and gave Natalie a look that told her she was going to stand there until she spilled.

"Christmas is coming." That pretty much said it all.

"What is this, *Game of Thrones*? Of course Christmas is coming. It's almost December, honey, and it's one of the more predictable holidays."

Natalie set down her tablet and frowned. Each year, the holidays were a challenge for her. Normally, she would try going on a trip to avoid all of it, but with the late wedding, she didn't have time. Staying home meant she'd have to resort to being a shut-in. She certainly wasn't interested in spending it with one of her parents and their latest spouses. The last time she did that, she'd called her mother's third husband by her second husband's name and that made for an awkward evening.

Natalie leaned back in the conference room chair and sighed. "It's bothering me more than usual this year." And it was. She didn't know why, but it was. Maybe it was the combination of all her friends being blissfully in love colliding with the holidays that was making it doubly painful.

"Are you taking a trip or staying home?" Gretchen asked.

"I'm staying home. I was considering a trip to Buenos Aires, but I don't have time. We squeezed Lily's last-minute wedding in on the Saturday before Christmas, so I'll be involved in that and not able to do the normal end-of-year paperwork until it's over."

"You're not planning to work over the shutdown, are you?" Gretchen planted her hands on her hips. "You don't have to celebrate, but by damn, you've got to take the time off, Natalie. You work seven days a week sometimes."

Natalie dismissed her concerns. Working didn't bother her as much as being idle. She didn't have a family to go home to each night or piles of laundry or housework that a man or child generated faster than she could clean. She liked her job. "I don't work the late hours you and Amelia do. I'm never here until midnight."

"It doesn't matter. You're still putting in too much time. You need to get away from all of this. Maybe go to a tropical island and have a fling with a sexy stranger."

At that, Natalie snorted. "I'm sorry, but a man is not the answer to my problems. That actually makes it worse."

"I'm not saying fall in love and marry the guy. I'm just saying to keep him locked in your hotel suite until the last New Year's firework explodes. What can a night or two of hot sex hurt?"

Natalie looked up at Gretchen and realized what was really bothering her. Colin's rejection from the night of the engagement party still stung. She hadn't told anyone about it, but if she didn't give Gretchen a good reason now, she'd ride her about it until the New Year. "It can hurt plenty when the guy you throw yourself at is your best friend's brother and he turns you down flat."

Gretchen's mouth dropped open and she sunk back down into her seat. "What? When did this happen?"

Natalie took a big sip of her soy chai latte before she answered. "I had too much chardonnay at Lily's engagement party and thought I'd take a chance on the big brother I'd lusted over since I'd hit puberty. To put it nicely, he declined. End of story. So no, I'm not really in the mood for a fling, either."

"Well that sucks," Gretchen noted.

"That's one way of putting it."

"On the plus side, you won't really have to see him again until the wedding day, right? Then you'll be too busy to care."

"Yep. I'll make sure I look extra good that day so he'll see what he missed."

"That's my girl. I'm going to go get these email invitations out."

Natalie nodded and watched Gretchen leave the room. She picked up her tablet and her drink, following her out the door to her office. Settling in at her desk, she pulled out a new file folder and wrote *Russell-Watson Wedding* on the tab. She needed to get everything prepared for their preliminary meeting this afternoon.

Staying busy would keep Christmas, and Colin, off her mind.

Colin pulled into the parking lot at From This Moment, his gaze instantly scanning over the lackluster shrubs out front. He knew it was winter, but they could certainly use a little more pizzazz for curb appeal.

He parked and went inside the facility. Stepping through the front doors, he knew instantly why Lily had insisted on marrying here. Their box holly hedges might have left something to be desired, but their focus was clearly on the interior. The inside was stunning with high ceilings, crystal chandeliers, tall fresh flower arrangements on the entryway table and arched entryways leading to various wings of the building. Mom would've loved it.

He looked down at his watch. It was a minute to one, so he was right on time for the appointment. Colin felt a little silly coming here today. Weddings weren't exactly his forte, but he was stepping up in his parents' place. When he'd married a year and a half ago, it had been a quick courthouse affair. If they'd opted for something more glamorous, he would've let Pam take the lead. Pam wasn't interested in that, though, and apparently, neither was his sister, Lily.

If she'd had her way, she and Frankie would've gone down to the courthouse, too. There was no reason to rush the nuptials, like Colin and Pam, but Lily just wanted to be done. She loved Frankie and she wanted to be Mrs. Watson as soon as possible. Colin had had to twist her arm into having an actual wedding, reminding her that their mother would be rolling over in her grave if she knew what Lily was planning.

She'd finally agreed under two circumstances: one, that the wedding be at Natalie's facility. Two, that he handle all the details. He insisted on the wedding, he'd offered to pay for it; he could make all the decisions.

Lily intended to show up in a white dress on the big day and that was about it.

Colin wasn't certain how he'd managed to be around so many women who weren't interested in big weddings. Pam hadn't wanted to marry at all. Hell, if it hadn't been for the baby and his insistence, she wouldn't have accepted the proposal. In retrospect, he realized why she was so hesitant, but with Lily, it just seemed to be a general disinterest in tradition.

He didn't understand it. Their parents had been very traditional people. Old-fashioned, you might even say. When they died in a car accident, Colin had tried to keep the traditions alive for Lily's sake. He'd never imagined he would end up raising his younger sister when he was only nineteen, but he was determined to do a good job and not disappoint his parents' memory.

Lily was just not that concerned. To her, the past was the past and she wasn't going to get hung up on things like that. Formal weddings fell into the bucket of silly traditions that didn't matter much to her. But it mattered to him, so she'd relented.

Colin heard a door open down one of the hallways and a moment later he found himself once again face-to-face with Natalie Sharpe. She stopped short in the archway of the foyer, clutching a tablet to her gray silk blouse. Even as a teenager, she'd had a classic beauty about her. Her creamy skin and high cheekbones had drawn his attention even when she was sporting braces. He'd suppressed any attraction he might have had for his little sister's friend, but he'd always thought she would grow up into a beautiful woman. At the party, his suspicions had been confirmed. And better yet, she'd looked at him with a seductive smile and an openness he hadn't expected. They weren't kids anymore, but there were other complications that had made it impossible to take her up on her offer, as much as he regretted it.

Today, the look on her face was a far cry from that night. Her pink lips were parted in concern, a frown lining her brow. Then she took a breath and shook it off. She tried to hide her emotions under a mask of professionalism, but he could tell she wasn't pleased to see him.

"Colin? I wasn't expecting to see you today. Is something going on with Lily?"

"Lots of things are going on with Lily," he replied, "but not what you're implying. She's fine. She's just not interested in the details."

Natalie swung her dark ponytail over her shoulder, her nose wrinkling. "What do you mean?"

"I mean, she told me this is my show and I'm to plan it however I see fit. So here I am," he added, holding out his arms.

He watched Natalie try to process the news. Apparently Lily hadn't given her a heads-up, but why would she? He doubted Lily knew about their encounter at the engagement party. She wasn't the kind of girl to give much thought to how her choices would affect other people.

"I know this is an unusual arrangement, but Lily is an unusual woman, as you know."

That seemed to snap Natalie out of her fog. She nodded curtly and extended her arm. "Of course. Come this way to my office and we can discuss the details."

Colin followed behind her, appreciating the snug fit of her pants over the curve of her hips and rear. She was wearing a pair of low heels that gave just enough lift to flatter her figure. It was a shame she walked in such a stiff, robotic way. He wouldn't mind seeing those hips sway a little bit, but he knew Natalie was too uptight for that. She'd always been a sharp contrast to his free-spirited sister—no-nonsense, practical, serious. She walked like she was marching into battle, even if it was a simple trip down the hallway.

After their encounter at the engagement party, he'd started to wonder if there was a more relaxed, sensual side to her that he hadn't had the pleasure of knowing about. He could only imagine what she could be like if she took down that tight ponytail, had a glass of wine and relaxed for once.

He got the feeling he would know all about that if he'd accepted her offer at the party. Unfortunately, his rocky on-again, off-again relationship with Rachel had been *on* that night. As much as he might have wanted to spend private time with Natalie, he couldn't. Colin was not the kind of man who cheated, even on a rocky relationship. Especially after what had happened with Pam.

After realizing how much more he was attracted to Natalie than the woman he was dating, he'd broken it off with Rachel for good. He was hopeful that now that he was a free man, he might get a second chance with Natalie. So far the reception was cold, but he hoped she'd thaw to his charms in time.

He followed her into her office and took a seat in the guest chair. Her office was pleasantly decorated, but extremely tidy and organized. He could tell every knickknack had its place, every file had a home.

"Can I get you something to drink? We have bottled water, some sparkling juices and ginger ale."

That was an unexpected option. "Why do you have ginger ale?"

"Sometimes the bride's father gets a little queasy when he sees the estimate."

Colin laughed. "Water would be great. I'm not that worried about the bill."

Natalie got up, pulling two bottles of water out of the small stainless steel refrigerator tucked into her built-in bookshelves. "On that topic, what number makes you comfortable in terms of budget for the wedding?" she asked as she handed him a bottle.

Colin's fingers brushed over hers as he took the bottle from her hand. There was a spark as they touched, making his skin prickle with pins and needles as he pulled away. He clutched the icy cold water in his hand to dull the sensation and tried to focus on the conversation, instead of his reaction to a simple touch. "Like I said, I'm not that worried about it. My landscaping company has become extremely successful, and I want this to be an event that my parents would've thrown for Lily if they were alive. I don't think we need ridiculous extras like ice bars with martini luges, but in terms of food and decor, I'm all in. A pretty room, pretty flowers, good food, cake, music. The basics."

Natalie had hovered near her chair after handing him the water, making him wonder if she'd been affected by their touch, too. After listening to him, she nodded curtly and sat down. She reached for her tablet and started making careful notes. "How many guests are you anticipating? Lily provided me a list of emails, but we weren't sure of the final total."

"Probably about a hundred and fifty people. We've

got a lot of family and friends of my parents that would attend, but Frankie doesn't have many people nearby."

He watched her tap rapidly at her screen. "When I spoke with Lily, I suggested a winter wonderland theme and she seemed to like that. Is that agreeable?"

"Whatever she wants." Colin had no clue what a winter wonderland wedding would even entail. White, he supposed. Maybe some fake snow like the kind that surrounded Santa at the mall?

"Okay. Any other requests? Would you prefer a DJ or a band for the reception?"

That was one thing he had an answer for. "I'd like a string quartet, actually. Our mother played the violin and I think that would be a nice nod to her. At least for the ceremony. For the reception, we probably need something more upbeat so that Lily and her friends can dance and have a good time."

"How about a swing band? There's a great one locally that we've used a couple times."

"That would work. I think she mentioned going swing dancing at some club a few weeks back."

Natalie nodded and finally set down her tablet. "I'm going to have Amelia put together a suggested menu and some cake designs. Gretchen will do a display of the tablescape for your approval. I'll speak with our floral vendor to see what she recommends for the winter wonderland theme. We'll come up with a whole wedding motif with some options and we'll bring you back to review and approve all the final choices. We should probably have something together by tomorrow afternoon."

She certainly knew what she was doing and had this whole thing down to a science. That was good because Colin wasn't entirely sure what a tablescape even was.

He was frankly expecting this process to be a lot more painful, but perhaps that was the benefit of an all-in-one facility. "That all sounds great. Why don't you firm up those details with the other ladies and maybe we can meet for dinner tomorrow night to discuss it?"

Natalie's dark gaze snapped up from her tablet to meet his. "Dinner won't be necessary. We can set up another appointment if your schedule allows."

Colin tried not to look disappointed at her quick dismissal of dinner. He supposed he deserved that after he'd done the same to her last week. Perhaps she was just angry with him over it. If he could convince her to meet with him, maybe she could relax and he could explain to her what had happened that night. He got the distinct impression she wouldn't discuss it here at work.

"If not dinner, how about I just stop by here tomorrow evening? Do you mind staying past your usual time?"

Natalie snorted delicately and eased up out of her chair. "There's no usual time in this business. We work pretty much around the clock. What time should I expect you?"

"About six."

"Great," she said, offering her hand to him over the desk.

Colin was anxious to touch her again and see if he had the same reaction to her this time. He took her hand, enveloping it in his own and trying not to think about how soft her skin felt against his. There was another sizzle of awareness and this time, it traveled up his arm as he held her hand, making him all the more sorry she'd turned down his dinner invitation. He'd never had that instant of a reaction just by touching someone. He had this urge to lean into her and draw the scent of her perfume into his lungs even as the coil of desire in his gut tightened with every second they touched. What would it be like to actually kiss her?

He had been right before when he thought Natalie was caught off guard by their connection. He was certain he wasn't the only one to feel it. Colin watched as Natalie avoided his gaze, swallowed hard and gently extracted her hand from his. "Six it is."

Two

Discuss it over dinner? *Dinner!* Natalie was still steaming about her meeting with Colin the next afternoon. As she pulled together the portfolio for his review, she couldn't help replaying the conversation in her mind.

That look in his eye. The way he'd held her hand. Dinner! He was hitting on her. What was that about? Natalie was sorry, but that ship had sailed. Who was he to reject her, then come back a week later and change his mind? He had his shot and he blew it.

As she added the suggested menu to the file, she felt her bravado deflate a little. Natalie would be lying if she said she didn't want to take him up on the offer. She really, really did. But a girl had to draw the line somewhere. Her pride was at stake and if she came running just because he'd changed his mind, she'd look needy. She was anything but needy.

He had passed up on a one-night stand and what was done, was done. Now that she knew they were working together on the wedding plans, it was just as well. She didn't like to mix business with pleasure.

Natalie looked at the clock on her computer. It was almost six. The rest of the facility was dark and quiet. It was Tuesday, so the others were all off today. Natalie was supposed to be off, too, but she usually came into the office anyway. When it was quiet, she could catch up on paperwork and filing, talk with their vendors and answer the phone in case a client called. Or stopped by, as the case was tonight.

She slid open the desk drawer where she kept all her toiletries. Pulling out a small hand mirror, she checked her teeth for lipstick, smoothed her hand over her hair and admired her overall look. She found her compact to apply powder to the shinier areas and reapplied her lipstick. She may have put a little extra effort into her appearance today. Not to impress Colin. Not really. She did it more to torture him. Her pride stung from his rebuffing and she wanted him to suffer just a little bit, too.

Satisfied, she slipped her things back into the drawer. A soft door chime sounded a moment later and she knew that he'd arrived. She stood, taking a deep breath and willing herself to ignore her attraction to him. This was about work. Work. And anytime she thought differently, she needed to remind herself how she'd felt when he rejected her.

Natalie walked quickly down the hallway to the lobby. She found Colin waiting for her there. At the party and at their meeting yesterday, he'd been wearing a suit, but tonight, he was wearing a tight T-shirt and khakis. She watched the muscles of his broad shoulders move beneath the fabric as he slipped out of his winter coat, hanging it on the rack by the door.

When he turned to face her, she was blindsided by his bright smile and defined forearms. When he wore his suit, it was easy to forget he wasn't just a CEO, he was also a landscaper. She'd wager he rarely got dirt under his nails these days, but he still had the muscular arms and chest of a man who could move the earth with brute strength.

Colin looked down, seemingly following her gaze. "Do you like the shirt? We just had them made up for all the staff to wear when they're out on job sites."

Honestly, she hadn't paid much attention to the shirt, but talking about that was certainly better than admitting she was lusting over his hard pecs. "It's very nice," she said with a polite smile. "I like the dark green color." And she did. It had the Russell Landscaping logo in white on the front. It looked nice on him. Especially the fact that it looked painted on.

"Me, too. You didn't call to say there was an issue, so I assume you have the wedding plans ready?"

"I do. Come on back to my office and I'll show you what we've pulled together."

They turned and walked down the hallway, side by side. She couldn't help but notice that Colin had gently rested a guiding hand at the small of her back as she slipped into the office ahead of him. It was a faint touch, and yet she could still feel the heat of it through her clothes. Goose bumps raised up across her forearms when he pulled away, leaving her cold. It was an unexpected touch and yet she had to admit she was a little disappointed it was so quick. Despite their years apart, her reaction to Colin had only grown along with his biceps. Unfortunately, those little thrills were all she'd allow herself to have. She was first and foremost a professional.

They settled into her office and Natalie pulled out the trifold portfolio she used for these meetings. She unfolded it, showing all the images and options for their wedding. Focusing on work was her best strategy for dealing with her attraction to Colin.

"Let's start with the menu," she began. "Amelia, our caterer, would normally do up to three entrees for a wedding this size, but with such short notice, we really don't have time for attendees to select their meals. Instead, she put together a surf and turf option that should make everyone happy. Option one pairs her very popular beef tenderloin with a crab cake. You also have the choice of doing a bourbon-glazed salmon, or a chicken option instead if you think fish might be a problem for your guests."

She watched Colin look over the options thoughtfully. She liked the way his brow drew together as he thought. Staring down at the portfolio, she could see how long and thick his eyelashes were. Most women would kill for lashes like those.

"What would you choose?" he asked, unaware of her intense study of his face.

"The crab cake," Natalie said without hesitation. "They're almost all crab, with a crisp outside and a spicy remoulade. They're amazing."

"Okay, that sounds great. Let's go with that."

Natalie checked off his selection. "For the cake, she put together three concept designs." She went into detail on each, explaining the decorations and how it fit with the theme.

When she was finally done, he asked again, "Which one of these cakes would you choose?"

Natalie wasn't used to this. Most brides knew exactly what they wanted. Looking down at the three concept sketches for the cake, she pointed out the second option. "I'd choose this one. It will be all white with an iridescent shimmer to the fondant. Amelia will make silver gum paste snowflakes and when they wrap around the cake it will be really enchanting."

"Let's go with that one. What about cake flavors?"

"You won't make that decision today. If you can come Thursday, Amelia will set up a tasting session. She's doing a couple other appointments that day, so that would work best. Do you think Lily would be interested in coming to that?"

"I can work that out. I doubt Lily will join me, but I'll ask. I'm sure cake is cake in her eyes."

Natalie just didn't understand her friend at all. Natalie had no interest in marriage, therefore no interest in a wedding. But Lily should at least have the party she wanted and enjoy it. It didn't make sense to hand that over to someone else. Her inner control freak couldn't imagine someone else planning her wedding. If by some twist of fate, she was lobotomized and agreed to marry someone, she would control every last detail.

"Okay." Natalie noted the appointment in her tablet so Amelia could follow up with him on a time for Thursday. From there, they looked at some floral concepts and bouquet options. With each of them, he asked Natalie's opinion and went with that. Sitting across from her was a sexy, intelligent, wealthy, thoughtful and agreeable man. If she *was* the kind to marry, she'd crawl into his lap right now. Whoever did land Colin would be very lucky. At least for a while.

Everything flowed easily from there. Without much debate, they'd settled on assorted tall and low arrangements with a mix of white flowers including rose, ranunculus, stephanotis and hydrangea. It was everything she would've chosen and probably as close as she'd get to having a wedding without having to get married.

"Now that we've handled all that, the last thing I want to do is to take you to the table setup Gretchen put together."

They left her office and walked down to the storage room. She kept waiting for him to touch her again, but she was disappointed this time. Opening the doors, she let him inside ahead of her and followed him in. In their storage room, amongst the shelves of glassware, plates, silver vases and cake stands, they had one round dinner table set up. There, Gretchen put together mock-ups of the reception tables for brides to better visualize them and make changes.

"Gretchen has selected a soft white tablecloth with a delicate silver overlay of tiny beaded snowflakes. We'd carry the white and silver into the dishes with the silver chargers, silver-rimmed white china, and then use silver-and-glass centerpieces in a variety of heights. We'll bring in tasteful touches of sparkle with some crystals on white manzanita branches and lots of candles."

Colin ran the tip of his finger over a silver snowflake and nodded. "It all looks great to me. Very pretty. Gretchen has done a very nice job with it."

Natalie made a note in her tablet and shook her head with amazement. "You're the easiest client I've ever had. I refuse to believe it's really that easy. What are you hiding from me?"

Colin looked at her with a confused expression. "I'm not hiding anything. I know it isn't what you're used to, but really, I'm putting this wedding in your capable hands."

He placed his hand on her shoulder as he spoke. She could feel the heat radiating through the thin fabric of her cashmere sweater, making her want to pull at the collar as her internal temperature started to climb.

"You knew my parents. You know Lily. You've got the experience and the eye for this kind of thing. Aside from the discussion about flowers, I've had no clue what you were talking about most of the time. I just trust you to do a great job and I'll write the check."

Natalie tried not to frown. Her heated blood wasn't enough for her to ignore his words. He was counting on her. That was a lot of pressure. She knew she could pull it off beautifully, but he had an awful lot of confidence in her for a girl he hadn't seen since she wore a retainer to bed. "So would you rather just skip the cake tasting?"

"Oh no," he said with a smile that made her knees soften beneath her. "I have a massive sweet tooth, so I'm doing that for sure."

Natalie wasn't sure how much her body could take of being in close proximity to Colin as friends. She wanted to run her hand up his tanned, muscular forearm and rub against him like a cat. While she enjoyed indulging her sexuality from time to time, she didn't have a reaction like this to just any guy. It was unnerving and *so* inappropriate. This wedding couldn't come fast enough.

* * *

"Thank you for all your help with this," Colin said as Natalie closed up and they walked toward the door.

"That's what I do," she said with the same polite smile that was starting to make him crazy. He missed her real one. He remembered her carefree smile from her younger days and her seductive smile from the engagement party. This polite, blank smile meant nothing to him.

"No, really. You and your business partners are going out of your way to make this wedding happen. I don't know how to thank you."

Natalie pressed the alarm code and they stepped outside where she locked the door. "You and Lily are like family to me. Of course we'd do everything we could. Anyway, it's not like we're doing it for free. You're paying us for our time, so no worries."

Their cars were the only two in the parking lot, so he walked her over to the cherry-red two-seat Miata convertible. Had there been another car in the lot, he never would've guessed this belonged to Natalie. It had a hint of wild abandon that didn't seem to align with the precise and businesslike Natalie he knew. It convinced him more than ever that there was another side to her that he desperately wanted to see.

"Let me take you to dinner tonight," he said, nearly surprising himself with the suddenncss of it.

Natalie's dark brown eyes widened. "I really can't, Colin, but I appreciate the offer."

Two up at bats, two strikeouts. "Even just as friends?"

Her gaze flicked over his face and she shook her head. "You and I both know it wouldn't be as friends."

Turning away, Natalie unlocked her car and opened the door to toss her bag inside.

"I think that's unfair."

"Not really. Listen, Colin, I'm sorry about the other night at the party. I'd been hit by a big dose of nostalgia and too much wine and thought that indulging those old teenage fantasies was a good idea. But by the light of day, I know it was silly of me. So thank you for having some sense and keeping me from doing something that would've made this whole planning process that much more awkward."

"Don't thank me," Colin argued. "I've regretted that decision every night since it happened."

Natalie's mouth fell agape, her dark eyes searching his face for something. "Don't," she said at last. "It was the right choice."

"It was at the time, but only because it had to be. Natalie, I—"

"Don't," Natalie insisted. "There's no reason to explain yourself. You made the decision you needed to make and it was the right one. No big deal. I'd like to just put that whole exchange behind us. The truth is that I'm really not the right kind of woman for you."

Colin wasn't sure if she truly meant what she said or if she was just angry with him, but he was curious what she meant by that. He was bad enough at choosing women. Maybe she knew something he didn't. "What kind of woman is that?"

"The kind that's going to have any sort of future with you. At the party, I was just after a night of fun, nothing serious. You're a serious kind of guy. Since you were a teenager, you were on the express train to marriage and kids. I'm on a completely different track."

They hadn't really been around each other long enough for Colin to think much past the ache of desire she seemed to constantly rouse in him. But if what she said was true, she was right. He wanted all those things. If she didn't, there wasn't much point in pursuing her. His groin felt otherwise, but it would get on board eventually.

"Well, I appreciate you laying that out for me. Not all women are as forthcoming." Pam had been, but for some reason he'd refused to listen. This time he knew better than to try to twist a woman's will. It didn't work. "Just friends, then," he said.

Natalie smiled with more warmth than before, and she seemed to relax for the first time since he'd arrived. "Friends is great."

"All right," he said. "Good night." Colin leaned in to give Natalie a quick hug goodbye. At least that was the idea.

Once he had his arms wrapped around her and her cheek pressed to his, it was harder to let go than he expected. Finally, he forced himself back, dropping his hands at his sides and breaking the connection he'd quickly come to crave. And yet, he couldn't get himself to say good-night and go back to his truck. "Listen, before you go can I ask you about something?"

"Sure," she said, although there was a hesitation in her voice that made him think she'd much rather flee than continue talking to him in the cold. She must not think he'd taken the hint.

"I'm thinking about giving Lily and Frankie the old house as a wedding present."

"The house you and Lily grew up in?" she asked with raised brows.

"Yes. It's been sitting mostly empty the last few years. Lily has been living with Frankie in the little apartment over his motorcycle shop. They seem to think that's great, but they're going to need more space if they want to start a family."

"That's a pretty amazing wedding present. Not many people register for a house."

Colin shrugged. "I don't need it. I have my place. It's paid for, so all they'd have to worry about are taxes and insurance. The only problem is that it needs to be cleaned out. I never had the heart to go through all of Mom's and Dad's things. I want to clear all that out and get it ready for the newlyweds to make a fresh start there."

Natalie nodded as he explained. "That sounds like a good plan. What does it have to do with me?"

"Well," Colin said with an uncharacteristically sheepish smile, "I was wondering if you would be interested in helping me."

She flinched at first, covering her reaction by shuffling her feet in the cold. "I don't know that I'll be much help to you, Colin. For one thing, I'm a wedding planner, not an interior decorator. And for another thing, I work most of the weekends with weddings. I don't have a lot of free time."

"I know," he said, "and I'm not expecting any heavy lifting on your part. I was thinking more of your organizational skills and keen aesthetic eye. It seems to me like you could spot a quality piece of furniture or artwork that's worth keeping amongst the piles of eighties-style recliners."

There was a light of amusement in her eyes as she

listened to him speak. "You're completely in over your head with this one, aren't you?"

"You have no idea. My business is landscaping, and that's the one thing at the house that doesn't need any work. I overhauled it a few years ago and I've had it maintained, so the outside is fine. It's just the inside. I also thought it would be nice to decorate the house for Christmas since they get back from their honeymoon on Christmas Eve. That way it will be ready to go for the holidays."

The twinkle in her eye faded. "I'm no good with Christmas, Colin. I might be able to help you with some of the furniture and keepsakes, but you're on your own when it comes to the holidays."

That made Colin frown. Most people enjoyed decorating for Christmas. Why was she so opposed to it? In his eyes it wasn't much different from decorating for a wedding. He wasn't about to push that point, however. "Fair enough. I'm sure I can handle that part on my own. Do you have plans tonight?"

Natalie sighed and shook her head. "I'm *not* going out with you, Colin."

He held up his hands in surrender. "I didn't ask you out. I asked if you were busy. I thought if you weren't busy, I'd take you by the old house tonight. I know you don't have a lot of free time, so if you could just take a walk through with me this evening and give me some ideas, I could get started on it."

"Oh," she said, looking sheepish.

"I mean, I could just pay a crew to come and clean out the house and put everything in storage, but I hate to do that. Some things are more important than others, and I'll want to keep some of it. Putting everything in storage just delays the inevitable. I could use your help, even if for just tonight."

Natalie sighed and eventually nodded. "Sure. I have some time tonight."

"Great. We'll take my car and I'll bring you back when we're done," Colin said.

He got the distinct impression that if he let Natalie get in her car, she'd end up driving somewhere other than their old neighborhood, or make some excuse for a quick getaway. He supposed that most men agreed to just being friends, but secretly hoped for more. Colin meant what he'd said and since she'd agreed, there was no need to slink away with his tail between his legs.

Holding out his arm, he ushered her reluctantly over to his Russell Landscaping truck. The Platinum series F-250 wasn't a work truck, it was more for advertising, although he did get it dirty from time to time. It was dark green, like their shirts, with the company logo and information emblazoned on the side.

He held the passenger door open for her, a step automatically unfolding along the side of the truck. Colin held her hand as she climbed inside, then slammed the door shut.

"Do you mind if we listen to some music on the way?" she asked.

Colin figured that she wanted music to avoid idle conversation, but he didn't mind. "Sure." He turned on the radio, which started playing music from the holiday station he'd had on last.

"Can I change it to the country channel?"

"I don't care, although you don't strike me as a country girl," he noted.

"I was born and raised in Nashville, you know. When

I was a kid, my dad would take me to see performances at the Grand Ole Opry. It's always stuck with me." She changed the station and the new Blake Wright song came on. "Ooh. I love this song. He's going to be doing a show at the Opry in two weeks. It's sold out, though."

Colin noted that information and put it in his back pocket. From there, it wasn't a long drive to the old neighborhood, just a few miles on the highway. Blake had just finished singing when they arrived.

They had grown up in a nice area—big homes on big lots designed for middle-class families. His parents honestly couldn't really afford their house when they had first bought it, but his father had insisted that they get the home they wanted to have forever. His parents had wanted a place to both raise their children and entertain potential clients, and appearances counted. If that meant a few lean years while the landscaping business built up, so be it.

The neighborhood was still nice and the homes had retained an excellent property value. It wasn't as flashy or trendy with the Nashville wealthy like Colin's current neighborhood, but it was a home most people would be happy to have.

As they pulled into the driveway, Natalie leaned forward and eyed the house through the windshield with a soft smile. "I've always loved this house," she admitted. "I can't believe how big the magnolia trees have gotten."

Colin's father had planted crepe myrtles lining the front walkway and magnolia trees flanking the yard. When he was a kid they were barely big enough to provide enough shade to play beneath them. Now the magnolias were as tall as the two-story roofline. "I've maintained the yard over the years," he said proudly. "I knew how important that was for Dad."

It was too dark to really get a good look at the outside, even with the lights on, so he opened the garage door and opted to take her in through there. His father's tool bench and chest still sat along the rear wall. A shed in the back housed all the gardening supplies and equipment. He hadn't had the heart to move any of that stuff before, but like the rest of it, he knew it was time.

They entered into the kitchen from the garage. Natalie instantly moved over to the breakfast bar, settling onto one of the barstools where she and Lily used to sit and do their homework together.

He could almost envision her with the braces and the braids again, but he much preferred Natalie as she was now. She smiled as she looked around the house, obviously as fond of his childhood home as he was. He wanted to walk up behind her to look at it the same way she was. Maybe rub the tension from her tight shoulders.

But he wouldn't. It had taken convincing to get her here. He wasn't about to run her off so quickly by pushing the boundaries of their newly established friendship. Eventually, it would be easier to ignore the swell of her breasts as they pressed against her sweater or the luminous curve of her cheek. Until then, he smoothed his hands over the granite countertop and let the cold stone cool his ardor.

"How long has it been since you've lived here, Colin? It seems pretty tidy."

"It's been about three years since I lived here full-time. Lily used it as a home base on and off for a while, but no one has really lived here for a year at least. I have a service come clean and I stop in periodically to check on the place."

"So many memories." She slipped off the stool and went into the living room. He followed her there, watching her look around at the vaulted ceilings. Natalie pointed at the loft that overlooked the living room. "I used to love hanging out up there, listening to CDs and playing on the computer."

That made him smile. The girls had always been sprawled out on the rug or lying across the futon up there, messing around on the weekends. Natalie had spent a lot of time at the house when they were younger. Her own house was only the next block over, but things had been pretty volatile leading up to her parents' divorce. While he hated that her parents split up, it had been nice to have her around, especially after his own parents died. Colin had been too busy trying to take care of everything and suddenly be a grown-up. Natalie had been there for Lily in a way he hadn't.

"Lily is very lucky to have a brother like you," she said, conflicting with his own thoughts. "I'm sure she'll love the house. It's perfect for starting a family. Just one thing, though."

"What's that?"

Natalie looked at him and smiled. "The house is exactly the same as it was the last time I was here ten years ago, and things were dated then. You've got some work ahead of you, mister."

Three

After a few hours at the house, Colin insisted on ordering pizza and Natalie finally acquiesced. That wasn't a dinner date, technically, and she was starving. She wasn't sure that he had put the idea of them being more than friends to bed—honestly neither had she—but they'd get there. As with all attractions, the chemical reactions would fade, the hormones would quiet and things would be fine. With a wedding and the house to focus on, she was certain it would happen sooner rather than later.

While he dealt with ordering their food, she slipped out onto the back deck and sat down in one of the old patio chairs. The air was cold and still, but it felt good to breathe it in.

She was exhausted. They'd gone through every room, talking over pieces to keep, things to donate and what renovations were needed. It wasn't just that, though. It was the memories and emotions tied to the place that were getting to her. Nearly every room in the house held some kind of significance to her. Even though Lily and Colin's parents had been dead for nearly thirteen years now, Natalie understood why Colin had been so reluctant to change things. It was like messing with the past somehow.

Her parents' marriage had dissolved when she was fourteen. The year or so leading up to it had been even more rough on her than what followed. Lily's house had been her sanctuary from the yelling. After school, on the weekends, sleepovers…she was almost always here. Some of her happiest memories were in this place. Colin and Lily's parents didn't mind having her around. She suspected that they knew what was going on at her house and were happy to shelter her from the brunt of it.

Unfortunately, they couldn't protect her from everything. There was nothing they could do to keep Natalie's father from walking out on Christmas day. They weren't there to hold Natalie's hand as her parents fought it out in court for two years, then each remarried again and again, looking for something in another person they couldn't seem to find.

Her friends joked that Natalie was jaded about relationships, but she had a right to be. She rarely saw them succeed. Why would she put herself through that just because there was this societal pressure to do it? She could see the icy water and jagged rocks below; why would she jump off the bridge with everyone else?

She heard the doorbell and a moment later, Colin called her from the kitchen. "Soup's on!"

Reluctantly, Natalie got back up and went inside the

house to face Colin and the memories there. She found a piping hot pizza sitting on the kitchen island beside a bottle of white wine. "Did they deliver the wine, too?" she asked drily. The addition of wine to the pizza made this meal feel more suspiciously like the date she'd declined earlier. "If they do, I need their number. Wine delivery is an underserved market."

"No, it was in the wine chiller," he said as though it was just the most convenient beverage available. "I lived here for a few weeks after I broke up with Pam. It was left over."

Natalie had learned from Lily that Colin got a divorce earlier this year, but she didn't know much about the details. Their wedding had been a quiet affair and their divorce had been even quieter. All she did hear was that they had a son together. "I'm sorry to hear about your divorce. Do you still get to see your son pretty often?"

The pleasant smile slipped from his face. He jerked the cork out of the wine bottle and sighed heavily. "I don't have a son."

Natalie knew immediately that she had treaded into some unpleasant territory. She wasn't quite sure how to back out of it. "Oh. I guess I misheard."

"No. You heard right. Shane was born about six months after we got married." He poured them each a glass of chardonnay. "We divorced because I found out that Shane wasn't my son."

Sometimes Natalie hated being right about relationships. Bad things happened to really good people when the fantasy of love got in the way. She took a large sip of the wine to muffle her discomfort. "I'm sorry to hear that, Colin."

A smile quickly returned to his face, although it seemed a little more forced than before. "Don't be. I did it to myself. Pam had been adamant when we started dating that she didn't want to get married. When she told me she was pregnant, I thought she would change her mind, but she didn't. I think she finally gave in only because I wouldn't let it go. I should've known then that I'd made a mistake by forcing her into it."

Natalie stiffened with a piece of pizza dangling from her hand. She finally released it to the plate and cleared her throat. "Not everyone is meant for marriage," she said. "Too many people do it just because they think that's what they're supposed to do."

"If someone doesn't want to get married, they shouldn't. It's not fair to their partner."

She slid another slice of pizza onto his plate. Instead of opting for the perfectly good dining room table, Natalie returned to her perch at the breakfast bar. That's where she'd always eaten at Lily's house. "That's why I've made it a policy to be honest up front."

Colin followed suit, handing her a napkin and sliding onto the stool beside her. "And I appreciate that, especially after what happened with Pam. You're right though. I'm the kind of guy that is meant for marriage. I've just got to learn to make better choices in women," he said. Pam had been his most serious relationship, but he had a string of others that failed for different reasons. "My instincts always seem to be wrong."

Natalie took a bite of her pizza and chewed thoughtfully. She had dodged a bullet when Colin turned her down at the engagement party. She'd only been looking for a night of nostalgic indulgence, but he was the kind of guy who wanted more. More wasn't something she could give him. She was a bad choice, too. Not lie-about-the-paternity-of-your-child bad, but definitely not the traditional, marrying kind he needed.

"Your sister doesn't seem to want to get married," Natalie noted, sending the conversation in a different direction. She'd never seen a more reluctant bride. That kind of woman wouldn't normally bother with a place like From This Moment.

"Actually, she's very eager to marry. It's the wedding and the hoopla she can do without."

"That's an interesting reversal. A lot of women are more obsessed with the wedding day than the actual marriage."

"I think she'll appreciate it later, despite how much she squirms now. Eloping at the courthouse was very underwhelming. We said the same words, ended up just as legally joined in marriage, but it was missing a certain something. I want better for my little sister's big day."

"She'll get it," Natalie said with confidence. "We're the best."

They ate quietly for a few moments before Colin finished his slice and spoke up. "See," he said as he reached for another piece and grinned. "I told you that you'd have dinner with me eventually."

Natalie snorted softly, relieved to see the happier Colin return. "Oh, no," she argued with a smile. "This does not count, even if you add wine. Having dinner together implies a date. This is not a date."

Colin leaned his elbows on the counter and narrowed his eyes at her. "Since we're sharing tonight, do you mind telling me why you were so unhappy to see me yesterday at the chapel?"

"I wouldn't say unhappy. I would say surprised. I expected Lily. And considering what happened the last time I saw you, I was feeling a little embarrassed."

"Why?"

"Because I hit on you and failed miserably. It was stupid of me. It was a momentary weakness fueled by wine and abstinence. And since you passed up the chance, this is definitely not a date. We're on a nondate eating pizza at your childhood home."

A knowing grin spread across Colin's face, making Natalie curious, nervous and making her flush at the same time. "So that's what it's really about," he said with a finger pointed in her direction. "You were upset because I turned you down that night at the party."

Natalie's cheeks flamed at the accusation. "Not at all. I'm relieved, really." She took a large sip of her wine and hoped that sounded convincing enough.

"You can say that, but I know it isn't true. You couldn't get out of the house fast enough that night."

"I had an early day the next morning."

Colin raised his brow in question. He didn't believe a word she said. Neither did she.

"Okay, fine. So what?" she challenged. "So what if I'm holding it against you? I'm allowed to have feelings about your rejection."

"Of course you're allowed to have feelings. But I didn't reject you, Natalie."

"Oh really? What would you call it?"

Colin turned in his seat to face her, his palms resting on each knee. "I would call it being the good guy even when I didn't want to be. You may not have noticed, but I had a date at the party. She was in a corner sulking most of the night. It wasn't really serious and we broke it off the next day, but I couldn't very well ditch her and disappear with you."

Natalie's irritation started to deflate. She slumped in her seat, fingering absentmindedly at her pizza crust. "Oh."

"Oh," he repeated with a chuckle. "Now if you were the kind of woman that *would* date me, you'd be feeling pretty silly right now."

Natalie shook her head. "Even if I were that woman, this is still not a date. You can't just decide to be on a date halfway through an evening together. There's planning and preparation. You'd have to take me someplace nicer than this old kitchen, and I would wear a pretty dress instead of my clothes from work. A date is a whole experience."

"Fair enough," Colin agreed, taking another bite of his pizza. "This isn't a date."

Natalie turned to her food, ignoring the nervous butterflies that were fluttering in her stomach. It wasn't a date, but it certainly felt like one.

They cleaned up the kitchen together and opted to climb in the attic to take a look at what was up there before they called it a night. Colin's father had had the attic finished when they moved in, so the space was a little dusty, but it wasn't the treacherous, cobweb-filled space most attics were.

"Wow," Natalie said as she reached the top of the stairs. "There's a lot of stuff up here."

She was right. Colin looked around, feeling a little intimidated by the project he'd put on himself. He'd put all this off for too long, though. Giving the house to Lily and Frankie was the right thing to do and the motivation he needed to actually get it done.

He reached for a plastic tote and peeked inside. It was filled with old Christmas decorations. After further investigation, he realized that was what the majority of the items were. “My parents always went all out at Christmas,” he said. “I think we’ve found their stash.”

There were boxes of garland, lights, ornaments and lawn fixtures. A five-foot, light-up Santa stood in the corner beside a few white wooden reindeer that lit up and moved.

“This is what you were looking for, right?” Natalie asked. “You said you wanted to decorate the house for the holidays.”

He nodded and picked up a copy of *A Visit From St. Nicholas* from one of the boxes. His father had read that to them every year on Christmas Eve, even when he and his sister were far too old for that sort of thing. In the years since they’d passed, Colin would’ve given anything to sit and listen to his father read that to him again.

“This is perfect,” he said. “I have to go through all this to see what still works, but it’s a great start. I’ll just have to get a tree for the living room. What do you think?”

Natalie shrugged. “I told you before, I’m not much of an expert on Christmas.”

He’d forgotten. “So, what’s that about, Grinch?”

“Ha-ha,” she mocked, heading toward the stairs.

Colin snatched an old Santa’s hat out of a box and followed her down. He slipped it on. “Ho-ho-ho!” he shouted in his jolliest voice. “Little girl, tell Santa why you don’t like Christmas. Did I forget the pony you asked for?”

Natalie stopped on the landing and turned around to look at him. She tried to hide her smirk with her hand, but the light in her eyes gave away her amusement. "You look like an idiot."

"Come on," he insisted. "We've already talked about my matrimonial betrayal. It can't be a bigger downer than that."

"Pretty close," Natalie said, crossing her arms defensively over her chest. "My dad left on Christmas day."

The smile faded from his face. He pulled off the Santa hat. "I didn't know about that."

"Why would you? I'm sure you were spared the messy details."

"What happened?"

"I'm not entirely sure. They'd been fighting a bunch leading up to Christmas, but I think they were trying to hold it together through the holidays. That morning, we opened presents and had breakfast, the same as usual. Then, as I sat in the living room playing with my new Nintendo, I heard some shouting and doors slamming. The next thing I know, my dad is standing in the living room with his suitcases. He just moved out right then. I haven't celebrated Christmas since that day."

"You haven't celebrated at all? In fifteen years?"

"Nope. I silently protested for a few holidays, passed between parents, but once I went to college, it was done. No decorations, no presents, no Christmas carols."

He was almost sorry he'd asked. So many of Colin's favorite memories had revolved around the holidays with his parents. Even after they died, Christmas couldn't be ruined. He just worked that much harder to make it special for Lily. He'd always dreamed of the day he'd celebrate the holidays with his own family. He'd gotten a taste of it when they celebrated Shane's first Christmas, but not long after that, he learned the truth about his son's real father.

"That's the saddest thing I've ever heard." And coming from a guy whose life had fallen apart in the past year, that was saying a lot.

"Divorce happens," Natalie said. A distant, almost ambivalent look settled on her face. She continued down the stairs to the ground floor. "It happens to hundreds of couples every day. It happened to you. Heck, it's happened to my mother three times. She's on her fourth husband. My sad story isn't that uncommon."

"I actually wasn't talking about the divorce." Colin stepped down onto the first-floor landing and reached out to grip the railing. "I mean, I'm sure it was awful for you to live through your parents' split. I just hate that it ruined Christmas for you. Christmas is such a special time. It's about family and friends, magic and togetherness. It's a good thing we've decided to just be friends because I could never be with someone who didn't like Christmas."

"Really? It's that important?"

"Yep. I look forward to it all year. I couldn't imagine not celebrating."

"It's easier than you think. I stay busy with work or I try to travel."

Colin could only shake his head. She wasn't interested in long-term relationships or holidays, both things most people seemed to want or enjoy. Her parents' divorce must've hit at a crucial age for her. He couldn't help reaching out to put a soothing arm around her shoulder. "You shouldn't let your parents' crap ruin your chances for having a happy holiday for the rest of your life."

"I don't miss it," she said, shying away from his touch, although she didn't meet his eyes when she said it.

He didn't fully believe her. Just like he didn't believe her when she said she wasn't interested in going on a date with him. She did want to, she was just stubborn and afraid of intimacy. As much as he might be drawn to Natalie, he wasn't going to put himself in that boat again. He was tired of butting his head against relationship brick walls. But even if they were just friends, he couldn't let the Christmas thing slide. It was a challenge unlike any he'd had in a while.

"I think I could make you like Christmas again."

Natalie turned on her heel to look at him. Her eyebrow was arched curiously. "No, you can't."

"You don't have much faith in me. I can do anything I put my mind to."

"Be serious, Colin."

"I am serious," he argued.

"You can't make me like Christmas. That would take a lobotomy. Or a bout of amnesia. It won't happen otherwise."

He took a step closer, moving into her space. "If you're so confident, why don't we wager on it?"

Her dark eyes widened at him and she stepped back. "What? No. That's silly."

"Hmm..." Colin said, leaning in. "Sounds to me like you're too chicken to let me try. You know you'll lose the bet."

Natalie took another step backward until her back

was pressed against the front door. "I'm not scared. I'm just not interested in playing your little game."

"Come on. If you're so confident, it won't hurt to take me up on it. Name your victor's prize. We're going to be spending a lot of time together the next two weeks. This will make it more...interesting."

Natalie crossed her arms over her chest. "Okay, fine. You're going to lose, so it really doesn't matter. You have until the wedding reception to turn me into a Christmas fan again. If I win the bet, you have to pay for me to spend Christmas next year in Buenos Aires."

"Wow. Steep stakes," Colin said.

Natalie just shrugged it off. "Are you confident or not?"

Nice. Now she'd turned it so he was the chicken. "Of course I'm confident. You've got it. I'll even fly you there first class."

"And what do you want if you win?"

A million different options could've popped into his mind in that moment, but there was only one idea that really stuck with him. "In return, if I win the bet, you owe me...a kiss."

Natalie's eyebrow went up. "That's it? A kiss? I asked for a trip to South America."

Colin smiled. "Yep, that's all I want." It would be a nice little bonus to satisfy his curiosity, but in the end, he was more interested in bringing the magic back to Christmas for her. Everyone needed that in their life. He held out his hand. "Shall we shake on it and make this official?"

Natalie took a cleansing breath and nodded before taking his hand. He enveloped it with his own, noting how cold she was to the touch. She gasped as he held her, her eyes widening. "You're so warm," she said.

"I was about to mention how cold you are. What's the matter? Afraid you're going to lose the bet?"

She gave a soft smile and pulled her hand from his. "Not at all. I'm always cold."

"It *is* Christmastime," Colin noted. "That just means you'll need to bundle up when we go out in search of some Christmas spirit."

She frowned, a crease forming between her brows. "We're both really busy, Colin. What if I just kiss you now? Will you let the whole thing drop?"

Colin propped his palm on the wall over her shoulder and leaned in until they were separated by mere inches. He brought his hand up to cup her cheek, running the pad of this thumb across her full bottom lip. Her lips parted softly, her breath quickening as he got closer. He had been right. She was attracted to him, but that just wasn't enough for her to want more.

"You can kiss me now if you want to," he said. "But there's no way I'm dropping this bet."

His hand fell to his side as a smirk of irritation replaced the expression on her face. This was going to be more fun than he'd expected.

"It's getting late. I'd better get you home."

He pulled away, noting the slight downturn of Natalie's lips as he did. Was she disappointed that he didn't kiss her? He'd never met a woman who sent such conflicting signals before. He got the feeling she didn't know what she wanted.

She didn't need to worry. They might just be friends, but he would kiss her, and soon. Colin had no intention of losing this bet.

Four

Natalie was on pins and needles all day Thursday knowing that Colin would be coming for the cake tasting that afternoon. She was filled with this confusing mix of emotions. First, there was the apprehension over their bet. Colin was determined to get her in the Christmas spirit. Wednesday morning when she'd stepped outside, she found a fresh pine wreath on her front door with a big red velvet bow.

She was tempted to take it down, but she wouldn't. She could withstand his attempts, but she knew the more she resisted, the more she would see of Colin. That filled her with an almost teenage giddiness—the way she used to feel whenever Colin would smile at her when they were kids. It made her feel ridiculous considering nothing was going to happen between the two of them, and frankly, it was distracting her from her work. Thank goodness this weekend's wedding was a smaller affair.

She was about to call the florist to follow up on the bride's last-minute request for a few additional boutonnieres when she noticed a figure lurking in her doorway. It was Gretchen.

Natalie pulled off her earpiece. "Yes?"

"So Tuesday night, I was meeting a friend for dinner on this side of town and I happened to pass by the chapel around nine that night. I noticed your car was still in the parking lot."

Natalie tried not to frown at her coworker. "You know I work late sometimes."

"Yeah, that's what I thought at first, too, but none of the lights were on. Then I noticed on your Outlook calendar that you had a late appointment to discuss the Russell-Watson wedding." A smug grin crossed Gretchen's face.

Natalie rolled her eyes. "It was nothing, so don't turn it into something. We finalized the plans for the wedding, that's all. Then he asked me for help with his wedding present for Lily. He's giving her a house."

"A house? Lord," Gretchen declared with wide eyes. "I mean, I know I'm engaged to a movie star and all, but I have a hard time wrapping my head around how rich people think."

"It's actually the home they grew up in. He asked me to help him fix it up for them."

Gretchen nodded thoughtfully. "Did you help him rearrange some of the bedroom furniture?"

"Ugh, no." Natalie searched around her desk for something to throw, but all she had was a crystal paperweight shaped like a heart. She didn't want to knock

Gretchen unconscious, despite how gratifying it might feel in the moment. "We just walked around and talked about what I'd keep or donate. Nothing scandalous. I'm sorry to disappoint you."

"Well, boo. I was hopeful that this guy would make it up to you for his cruel rebuffing at the engagement party."

"He didn't make it up to me, but he did explain why he'd turned me down. Apparently he had a date that night."

"And now?"

"And now they've broken up. But that doesn't change anything. We're just going to be friends. It's better this way. Things would've just been more…complicated if something had happened."

Gretchen narrowed her gaze at her. "And you helping him with the house now that he's single won't be complicated?"

Natalie swung her ponytail over her shoulder and avoided her coworker's gaze by glancing at her computer screen. There were no critical emails to distract her from the conversation.

"Natalie?"

"No, it won't," she said at last. "It's going to be fine. We've been family friends for years and that isn't going to change. I'm going to handle the wedding and help him with the house and everything will be fine. Great, really. I think it's just the distraction I need to get through the holidays this year."

Gretchen nodded as she talked, but Natalie could tell she wasn't convinced. Frankly, neither was Natalie. Even as she said the words, she was speaking to herself as much as to her friend. She certainly wasn't going to tell her that she was fighting her attraction to Colin like a fireman with a five-alarm inferno. Or that she'd gotten herself roped into a bet that could cost her not only a kiss, but a solid dose of the holidays she had just said she was avoiding.

"Okay, well, whatever helps you get through the holidays, hon."

"Thank you."

"Uh-oh. Speak of the devil," Gretchen said, peeking out Natalie's window.

"He's here?" Natalie said, perking up in her seat, eyes wide with panic. "He's early." She was automatically opening her desk drawer and reaching for her compact when she heard Gretchen's low, evil laugh.

"No, he's not. I lied. I just wanted to see how you'd react. I was right. You're so full of it, your eyeballs should be floating."

Natalie sat back in her chair, the panic quickly replaced by irritation. Her gaze fell on the drawer to the soft foam rose stress ball that the florist had given them. She picked it up and hurled it at Gretchen, who ducked just in time.

"Get out of my office!" she shouted, but Gretchen was already gone. Natalie could hear her cackling down the hallway. Thank goodness there weren't any customers in the facility this morning.

There would be several clients here after lunchtime, though. Amelia had three cake tastings on the schedule today, including with Colin.

Hopefully that would go better than just now. Gretchen had already called her on the ridiculous infatuation that had reignited. Amelia would likely be more tactful. She hoped. Natalie didn't think she'd been that obvious. In the end, nothing *had* happened. They'd finalized plans, she'd helped him with the house and they'd had pizza. They hadn't kissed. She had certainly wanted to.

It was hard to disguise the overwhelming sense of disappointment she felt when they had their near miss. Natalie had been certain he was about to kiss her. She thought maybe dangling that carrot would serve her on two levels: first that they could call off the silly bet, and second, that she'd finally fulfill her youthful fantasy of kissing the dashing and handsome Colin Russell.

Then…nothing. He knew what he was doing. He'd turned up the dial, gotten her primed, then left her hanging. He was not letting her out of the bet. It might be a painful two weeks until the wedding while he tried, but in the end, she'd get a nice trip to Argentina out of it.

Colin was well-intentioned, but he wasn't going to turn her into a jolly ol' elf anytime soon. It wasn't as though she wanted to be a Humbug. She'd tried on several occasions to get into the spirit, but it never worked. The moment the carols started playing in the stores, she felt her soul begin to shrivel inside her. Honey-glazed ham tasted like ash in her mouth.

With her parents' marriages in shambles and no desire to ever start a family of her own, there wasn't anything left to the season but cold weather and commercialism.

That said, she didn't expect Colin to lose this bet quietly. He would try his damnedest, and if last night was any indication, he was willing to play dirty. If that was the case, she needed to as well. It wouldn't be hard to deploy her own distracting countermeasures. The chemistry between them was powerful and could easily derail his focus. She wouldn't have to go too far—a seductive smile and a gentle touch would easily plant something other than visions of sugarplums in his head.

Natalie reached back into the drawer for the mirror she'd sought out earlier. She looked over her hair and reapplied her burgundy lipstick. She repowdered her nose, then slipped everything back into her desk. Glancing down at her outfit, she opted to slip out of her blazer, leaving just the sleeveless burgundy and hunter-green satin shell beneath it. It had a deep V-neck cut, and the necklace she was wearing today would no doubt draw the eye down to the depths of her cleavage.

Finally, she dabbed a bit of perfume behind her ears, on her wrists and just between her collarbones. It was her favorite scent, exotic and complex, bringing to mind perfumed silk tents in the deserts of Arabia. A guy she'd once dated had told her that perfume was like a hook, luring him closer with the promise of sex.

She took a deep breath of the fragrance and smiled. It was playing dirty, but she had a bet to win.

"I brought you a gift."

Colin watched Natalie look up at him from her desk with a startled expression. From the looks of it, she'd been deep into her work and lost track of time. She recovered quickly, sitting back in her chair and pulling off her headset. "Did you? What is it now? A light-up snowman? A three-foot candy cane?"

"Close." He whipped out a box from behind his back and placed it on her desk. "It's peppermint bark from a candy shop downtown."

Natalie smirked at the box, opening it to admire the

contents. "Are you planning to buy your way through this whole bet?"

"Maybe. Either way, it's cheaper than a first-class ticket to Buenos Aires."

"You added the first class part yourself, you know, when you were feeling cocky." She leaned her elbows on the desk and watched him pointedly.

His gaze was drawn to a gold-and-emerald pendant that dangled just at the dip of her neckline. The shadows hinted at the breasts just beyond the necklace. He caught a whiff of her perfume and felt the muscles in his body start to tense. What were they talking about? Cocky. Yes. That was certainly on point. "Do you like the wreath?" he asked, diverting the subject.

"It's lovely," she said, sitting back with a satisfied smile that made him think she was teasing him on purpose.

That was definitely a change from that night at the house. She'd been adamant about being the wrong kind of woman for him and that they should be friends. Now she was almost dangling herself in front of him. He couldn't complain about the view, but he had to question the motivation.

"It makes my entryway smell like a pine forest."

At least she hadn't said Pine-Sol. "You're supposed to say it smells like Christmas."

"I don't know what Christmas is supposed to smell like. When I was a kid, Christmas smelled like burned biscuits and the nasty floral air freshener my mom would spray to keep my grandmother from finding out she was smoking again."

Colin winced at her miserable holiday memories. It sounded as though her Christmas experiences sucked long before her dad left. His next purchase was going to be a mulling spice candle. "That is not what Christmas smells like. It smells like pine and peppermint, spiced cider and baking sugar cookies."

"Maybe in Hallmark stores," she said, pushing up from her chair and glancing at her watch. "But now we need to focus on cake, not sugar cookies."

Colin followed her into a sitting room near the kitchen. It had several comfortable wingback chairs and a loveseat surrounding a coffee table.

"Have a seat." Natalie gestured into the room.

"Are you joining me?" he asked as he passed near to her.

"Oh yes," she said with a coy smile. "I've just got to let Amelia know we're ready."

He stepped inside and Natalie disappeared down the hallway. He was happy to have a moment alone. The smell of her skin mingling with her perfume and that naughty smile was a combination he couldn't take much more of. At least not and keep his hands off her.

Something had definitely changed since Tuesday. Tuesday night, she'd been more open and friendly once he told her why he'd turned her down, but nothing like this. Not even when she'd leaned into him, thinking he was about to kiss her.

Perhaps she was trying to distract him. Did she think that keeping his mind occupied with thoughts of her would shift the focus away from bringing Christmas joy back into her life? This had all happened after the bet, so that had to be it. *Tricky little minx.* That was playing dirty after her big speech about how she wasn't the right kind of woman for him. Well, two could play at that game. If he was right, now that he knew her ploy he'd let her see how far she was willing to push it to win.

No matter what, he wouldn't let himself be ensnared by her feminine charms. They were oil and water that wouldn't mix. But that didn't mean he wouldn't enjoy letting her try. And it didn't mean he'd let himself lose sight of the bet in the process.

He heard a click of heels on wood and a moment later Natalie came back into the room. She settled onto the loveseat beside him. Before he could say anything, the caterer, Amelia, blew in behind her.

"Okay," Amelia said as she carried a silver platter into the room and placed it on the coffee table. "Time for some cake tasting. This is the best part of planning a wedding, I think. Here are five of our most popular cake flavors." She pointed her manicured finger at the different cubes of cake that were stacked into elegant pyramids. "There's a white almond sour cream cake, triple chocolate fudge, red velvet, pistachio and lemon pound cake. In the bowls, we've got an assortment of different fillings along with samples of both my butter-cream and my marshmallow fondant. The cake design you selected will work with either finish, so it's really just a matter of what taste you prefer."

"It all looks wonderful, Amelia. Thanks for putting this together."

"Sure thing. On this card, it has all the flavors listed along with some popular combinations you might like to try. For a wedding of your size, I usually recommend two choices. I can do alternating tiers, so if a guest doesn't one like flavor, they can always try the other. The variety is nice. Plus, it makes it easier to choose if you have more than one you love."

"Great," Colin said, taking the card from her and setting it on the table. He watched as the caterer shot a pointed look at Natalie on the couch beside him.

"And if you don't mind, since Natalie is here with you, I'm going to go clean up in the kitchen. I've got another cake to finish piping tonight."

Colin nodded. He was fine being alone with Natalie. That left the door open for her little games anyway. "That's fine. I'm sure you've got plenty to do. Thanks for fitting me in on such short notice."

"Thanks, Amelia," Natalie said. "If we have any questions about the cake, I'll come get you."

Amelia nodded and slipped out of the room. Colin watched her go, then turned back to the platter in front of them. "Where should we start?"

Natalie picked up the card from the table. "I'd go with Amelia's suggestions. She knows her cake."

"Great. What's first?"

"White almond sour cream cake with lemon curd."

They both selected small squares of cake from the plate, smearing them with a touch of the filling using a small silver butter knife. Colin wasn't a big fan of lemon, but even he had to admit this was one of the best bites of cake he'd ever had.

And it was just the beginning. They tried them all, mixing chocolate cake with chocolate chip mousse, lemon pound cake with raspberry buttercream and red velvet with whipped cream cheese. There were a million different combinations to choose from. He was glad he'd eaten a light lunch because by the time they finished, all the cake was gone and his suit pants were a bit tighter than they'd been when he sat down.

"I don't know how we're going to choose," he said

at last. "It was all great. I don't think there was a single thing I didn't like."

"I told you she did great work."

Colin turned to look at Natalie, noticing she had a bit of buttercream icing in the corner of her mouth. "Uh-oh."

"What?" Natalie asked with concern lining her brow.

"You've got a little..." his voice trailed off as he reached out and wiped the icing away with the pad of his thumb. "...frosting. I got it," he said with a smile.

Natalie looked at the icing on the tip of his thumb. She surprised him by grasping his wrist to keep him from pulling away. With her eyes pinned on his, she leaned in and gently placed his thumb in her mouth. She sucked off the icing, gliding her tongue over his skin. Colin's groin tightened and blood started pumping hard through his veins.

She finally let go, a sweet smile on her face that didn't quite match her bold actions. "I didn't want any to go to waste."

For once in his life, Colin acted without thinking. He lunged for her, capturing her lips with his and clutching at her shoulders. He waited for Natalie to stiffen or struggle away from him, but she didn't. Instead, she brought up her hands to hold his face close to her, as though she was afraid he might pull away too soon.

Her lips were soft and tasted like sweet vanilla buttercream. He'd had plenty of cake today, but he couldn't get enough of her mouth. There was no hesitation in her touch, her tongue gliding along his just as she'd tortured him with his thumb a moment ago.

Finally, he pulled away. It took all his willpower to do it, but he knew he needed to. This was a wedding chapel, not a hotel room. He didn't move far, though. His hand was still resting on Natalie's upper arm, his face mere inches from hers. She was breathing hard, her cheeks flushed as her hands fell into her lap.

He could tell that he'd caught her off guard at first with that kiss, but he didn't care. She'd brought that on herself with her distracting games. If her body was any indicator, she hadn't minded. She'd clung to him, met him measure for measure. For someone who thought they were unsuitable for each other, she'd certainly participated in that kiss.

He just wished he knew that she wanted to, and she wasn't just doing it as a distraction to help her win the bet. There was one way to find out. She wasn't good at hiding her initial emotional responses, so he decided to push a few buttons. "So, what do you think?" he asked.

Natalie looked at him with glassy, wide eyes. "About what?"

"About the cake. I'm thinking definitely the white cake with the lemon, but I'm on the fence about the second choice."

Natalie stiffened, the hazy bliss vanishing in an instant. He could tell that cake was not what she'd had on her mind in that moment. She'd let her little game go too far. He was glad he wasn't the only one affected by it.

"Red velvet," she said. She sniffed delicately and sat back, pulling away from him. Instantly, she'd transformed back into the uptight, efficient wedding planner. "It's a universal flavor. I'm told it's a Christmas classic, so it suits the theme. It's also one of my favorites, so admittedly I'm partial."

"Okay. The choices are made. Thanks for being so… helpful."

Natalie looked at him with a narrowed gaze that softened as the coy smile from earlier returned. "My pleasure."

Five

Monday afternoon, Colin made a stop by Frankie's motorcycle store on his way home from his latest work site.

When he'd first found out that his sister was dating a guy who looked more like a biker than a businessman, he'd been hesitant. Meeting Frankie and visiting his custom bike shop downtown had changed things. Yes, he had more tattoos than Colin could count and several piercings, but he was a talented artisan of his craft. The motorcycles he designed and built were metal masterpieces that earned a high price. Over the past year, Frankie's business had really started to take off. It looked like he and Lily would have a promising future together.

Slipping into the shop, Colin walked past displays of parts, gear and accessories to the counter at the back. Lily was sitting at the counter. Frankie had hired her to run the register, making the business a family affair. Living upstairs from the shop had made it convenient, but he couldn't imagine they had enough space to raise a family there or even stretch their legs.

"Hey, brother of mine," Lily called from the counter. "Can I interest you in a chopper?"

"Very funny." Colin laughed.

Lily came out from behind the counter to give him a hug. "If not for a bike, to what do I owe this visit?"

"Well, I thought you might want to know about some of the wedding plans Natalie and I have put together." Colin had a copy of the design portfolio to show her. He hoped that by showing her the designs, she would start getting more excited about the wedding.

Lily shrugged and drifted back to her post behind the counter. "I'm sure whatever you've chosen will be great."

"At least look at it," Colin said, opening the folder on the counter. "Natalie and her partners have worked really hard on putting together a beautiful wedding for you. We went with the winter wonderland theme you and Natalie discussed. For the cake, we chose alternating tiers of white almond sour cream cake with lemon curd filling and red velvet with cream cheese. Natalie said those were two of their most popular flavors, and they were both really tasty."

"Sounds great," Lily said, sitting back onto her stool. "I have no doubt that it will come together beautifully. As long as I have someone to marry us, it's fine by me. The rest of this is just a bonus."

"Have you ordered a dress yet?"

His sister shook her head. "No."

Colin frowned. "Lily, you don't have a dress?"

"I was just going to pull something from my closet. I have that white dress from my sorority induction ceremony."

"Are you serious? You've got to go get a wedding dress, Lily."

His sister shrugged again, sending Colin's blood pressure higher. He couldn't fathom how she didn't care about any of this. Pam hadn't been very interested in planning their wedding either. Since they were in a hurry, they'd ended up with a courthouse visit without frills. It was a little anticlimactic. He didn't want that for Lily, but she seemed indifferent about the whole thing.

"I've got a job, Colin. Frankie and I work at the shop six days a week. I can't go running around trying on fluffy Cinderella dresses. If you are so concerned with what I'm wearing, you can pick it out. I wear a size six. Natalie and I used to be able to share clothes when we were teenagers. At the engagement party she looked like she might still wear the same size as I do. I'm sure you two can work it out without me."

Colin fought the urge to drop his face into his hands in dismay. "Will you at least go to a dress fitting?"

"Yeah, sure."

"Okay. So we'll get a dress." He pulled out his phone to call Natalie and let her know the bad news. He knew she had been busy over the weekend with a wedding, so he hadn't bothered her with wedding or holiday details. He couldn't wait any longer, though. He was certain this was an important detail and could be the very thing that pushed his cool, calm and collected wedding planner over the edge.

She didn't answer, so he left a quick message on her

phone. When he slipped his phone back into his pocket, he noticed Lily watching him. "What?"

"Your voice changed when you left her a message."

"I was trying to soften the blow," he insisted.

Lily shook her head. "I don't know. That voice sounded like the same voice I remember from when you would tie up the house phone talking to girls in high school. What's going on between you two?"

"Going on?" Colin tried to find the best way to word it. "I don't know. We've spent a lot of time together planning the wedding. Things have been…interesting."

"Are you dating?"

"No," Colin said more confidently. He was determined not to wade into that territory with Natalie. She was beautiful and smart and alluring, but she also had it in her to crush him. "Natalie and I have very different ideas on what constitutes a relationship."

Lily nodded. "Natalie has never been the princess waiting for her prince to save her. She always kept it casual with guys. I take it you're not interested in a booty call. You should consider it. Going from serious relationship to serious relationship isn't working for you either."

Colin did not want to have this conversation with his little sister. Instead, he ignored the kernel of truth in her words. "I am not going to discuss booty calls with you. I can't believe I even said that phrase out loud."

"Have you kissed her?"

He didn't answer right away.

"Colin?"

"Yes, I kissed her."

Lily made a thoughtful clicking sound with her tongue. "Interesting," she said slowly, her hands planted on her hips. "What exactly do you—?"

Colin's phone started to ring at his hip, interrupting her query. He'd never been so relieved to get a call. "I've got to take this," he said, answering the phone and moving to the front of the shop. "Hello?"

"There's no dress?" It was Natalie, her displeasure evident by the flat tone of her query.

"That is correct," he said with a heavy sigh. "And like everything else, she says to just pick something. Lily says she's a size six and that you used to share clothes, so fake it."

"Fake it?" Natalie shrieked into his ear.

"Yep." He didn't know what else to say.

Natalie sat silent on the other end of the line for a moment. "I need to make a few calls. Can you meet me at a bridal salon tonight?"

Colin looked down at his watch. It was already after five. Did they have enough time? "Sure."

"Okay. I'll call you back and let you know where to meet me."

Colin hung up, turning to see a smug look on his sister's face.

"I told you she could handle it."

"That well may be, but she wasn't happy about it." At this point, they'd probably be lucky if Lily didn't go down the aisle in a white trash bag. They had about two weeks to pick the dress, order it, have it come in and do any alterations. He wasn't much of a wedding expert, but he got the feeling it would be a rough road. "What about Frankie? Do I need to dress him, too?"

Lily shook her head and Colin felt a wave of relief wash over him. "He's good. He's got a white suit and picked out a silver bowtie and suspenders to go with the theme."

He should've known a bit of hipster style would make its way into this wedding. Whatever. It was one less person he had to dress.

Returning to the counter, he closed the wedding portfolio. He was anxious to get out of here before Lily started up the conversation about Natalie again. "Okay, well, I'm off to meet Natalie at some bridal salon. Any other surprises you're waiting to tell me until an inopportune time?"

The slight twist of Lily's lips was proof that there was. "Well…" she hesitated. "I kind of forgot about this before, but it should be fine."

Somehow, he doubted that. "What, Lily?"

"Next week, Frankie and I are flying to Las Vegas for a motorcycle convention."

"Next week? Lily, the wedding is next week."

"The wedding isn't until Saturday. We're flying back Friday. No problem."

Colin dropped his forehead into his hand and squeezed at his temples. "What time on Friday? You've got the rehearsal that afternoon and the rehearsal dinner after that."

"Hmm…" she said thoughtfully, reaching for her phone. She flipped through the screens to pull up her calendar. "Our flight is scheduled to arrive in Nashville at one. That should be plenty of time, right?"

"Right." He didn't bother to point out that it was winter and weather delays were a very real concern this time of year. With his luck, she was connecting in Chicago or Detroit. "When do you leave?"

"Monday."

Colin nodded. Well, at the very least, he knew he

could work on the house without worrying about her stopping by and ruining the surprise.

A chime on his phone announced a text. Natalie had sent him the name and address of the bridal shop where they were meeting.

"Anything else I need to know, Lil?"

She smiled innocently, reminding him of the sweet girl with pigtails he remembered growing up. "Nope. That's it."

"Okay," he said, slipping his phone back into his pocket. "I'm off to buy you a wedding dress."

"Good luck," she called to him as he slipped out of the store.

He'd need it.

Natalie swallowed her apprehension as she went into the bridal shop. Not because she had to get Lily a dress at the last minute—that didn't surprise her at all. They were close enough to sample size to buy something out of the shop and alter it.

Really, she was more concerned about trying on wedding dresses. It wasn't for her, she understood that, but it still felt odd. She'd never tried on a wedding dress before, not even for fun. Her mother had sold her wedding dress when her parents divorced.

She knew it was just a dress, but there was something transformative about it. She didn't want to feel that feeling. That was worse than Christmas spirit.

She'd avoided the bulk of Colin's holiday bet by staying busy with a wedding all weekend. But now it was the start of a new week and she had no doubt he would find some way to slip a little Christmas into each day.

In addition to the wreath and the peppermint bark,

she'd also received a Christmas card that played carols when she opened it. A local bakery had delivered a fruitcake to the office on Friday, and a florist had brought a poinsettia on Saturday morning.

What he didn't know was that she'd received plenty of well-meaning holiday gifts throughout the years. That wasn't going to crack her. It just gave her a plant to water every other day.

As she entered the waiting room of the salon, she found Colin and the storekeeper, Ruby, searching through the tall racks of gowns. Ruby looked up as she heard Natalie approach.

"Miss Sharpe! There you are. Mr. Russell and I were looking through a few gowns while we waited."

"Not a problem. Thanks for scheduling us with such late notice."

"This is the bridal business," Ruby said with a dismissive chuckle. "You never know what you'll get. For every girl that orders her gown a year in advance, I get one pregnant and in-a-hurry bride that needs a gown right away. After being in this industry for twenty years, I've learned to keep a good stock of dresses on hand for times like this."

Ruby was good at what she did. Natalie referred a lot of brides to her salon because of it. "Did Colin fill you in on what we need?"

"Yes. He said you need something in a street size six that will fit a winter wonderland theme. He also said the bride won't be here to try them on."

"That's correct. We wear the same size, so I'll try on the dresses in her place."

"Okay. I'd recommend something with a corset back. You don't have a lot of time for alterations and with a corset bodice, you can tighten or loosen it to account for any adjustments in your sizes."

Brilliant. She'd have to remember this in the future for quick-turnaround brides. "Perfect."

"Great. If you'd like to take a seat, Mr. Russell, I'll take Miss Sharpe to the dressing room to try on a few gowns to see what you like."

"Have fun," Colin said, waving casually at her as she was ushered into the back.

She was officially on the other side now. She'd passed the curtain where only brides went. It made her stomach ache.

"I've pulled these three dresses to start with. I think you're pretty close to the sample size, so this should be a decent fit. Which would you like to try first?"

Natalie looked over the gowns with apprehension. She needed to think like Lily. Everything else about the wedding had turned out to be Natalie's choice, but when it came to dresses, it seemed wrong to pick something she liked. "It doesn't matter," she said. "I'm going to let her brother choose."

"Then let's start with the ruched satin gown."

Natalie slipped out of her blouse and pencil skirt and let Ruby slip the gown over her head. She was fully aware how heavy bridal gowns could be, but for some reason, it seemed so much heavier on than she had expected it to.

She held the gown in place as Ruby tightened the corset laces in the back. Looking in the mirror, she admired the fit of the gown. The corset gave her a curvy, seductive shape she hadn't expected. She never felt much like a sex kitten. Her shape had always been a little lanky and boyish in her opinion, but the gown changed that.

The decorative crystals that lined the sweetheart neckline drew the eyes to her enhanced cleavage.

"Do you like the snowflake?"

Natalie narrowed her gaze at her reflection and noticed the crystal design at her hip that looked very much like a snowflake. Perfect for the theme. "It's nice. It's got a good shape and the crystals give it a little shine without being overpowering."

"Let's go show him."

There was more apprehension as Natalie left the dressing room. This wasn't about her, but she wanted to look the best she could when she stepped onto the riser to show him the gown. She focused on her posture and grace as she glided out into the salon.

Her gaze met his the minute she cleared the curtain. His golden hazel eyes raked up and down the length of the gown with the same heat of appreciation she'd seen that night at the engagement party. Natalie felt a flush of heat rise to her cheeks as she stepped onto the pedestal for his inspection.

"It's beautiful," he said. "It's very elegant and you look amazing in it. But I have to say that it's not right for Lily at all."

Natalie sighed and looked down. He was right. "Ruby, do we have one that's a little more whimsical and fun?"

Ruby nodded and helped her down. "I have a few that might work. How fun are we talking?" she asked as they stepped back into the dressing room. "Crazy tulle skirt? Blush- or pink-colored gowns?"

"If she was here, probably all that and more. But she should've shown up herself if she had that strong of an opinion. Let's go for something a little more whimsical, but still classically bridal."

The minute Ruby held up the gown, Natalie knew this dress was the one. It was like something out of a winter fantasy—the gown of the snow queen. It was a fitted, mermaid style with a sweetheart neckline and sheer, full-length sleeves. All across the gown and along the sleeves were delicate white-and-silver-stitched floral designs that looked almost like glittering snowflakes dancing across her skin.

She held her breath as she slipped into the gown and got laced up. Ruby fastened a few buttons at her shoulders and then it was done. It was the most beautiful dress she'd ever seen, and she'd seen hundreds of brides come through the chapel over the years.

"This gown has a matching veil with the same lace trim along the edges. Do you want to go out there with it on?"

"Yes," she said immediately. Natalie wanted to see the dress with the veil. She knew it would make all the difference.

Ruby swiftly pinned her hair up and set the veil's comb in. The veil flowed all the way to floor, longer than even the gown's chapel-length train.

It was perfect. Everything she'd ever wanted.

Natalie swallowed hard. Everything she'd ever wanted *for Lily*, she corrected herself. Planning a wedding in the bride's place was messing with her head.

She headed back out to the salon. This time, she avoided Colin's gaze, focusing on lifting the hem of the skirt to step up on the pedestal. She glanced at herself for only a moment in the three-sided mirror, but even that was enough for the prickle of tears to form in her eyes.

Quickly, she jerked away, turning to face Colin. She covered her tears by fidgeting with her gown and veil.

"What do you think of this one?" Ruby asked.

The long silence forced Natalie to finally meet Colin's gaze. Did he hate it?

Immediately, she knew that was not the case. He was just stunned speechless.

"Colin?"

"Wow," he finally managed. He stood up from the velour settee and walked closer.

Natalie felt her chest grow tighter with every step. He wasn't looking at the gown. Not really. He was looking at her. The intensity of his gaze made her insides turn molten. Her knees started trembling and she was thankful for the full skirt that covered them.

Just when she thought she couldn't bear his gaze any longer, his eyes dropped down to look over the details of the dress. "This is the one. No question."

Natalie took a breath and looked down to examine the dress. "Do you think Lily will like it?"

Colin hesitated a moment, swallowing hard before he spoke. "I do. It will look beautiful on her. I don't think we could find a dress better suited to the theme you've put together." He took a step back and nodded again from a distance. "Let's get this one."

"Wonderful!" Ruby exclaimed. "This one really is lovely."

The older woman went to the counter to write up the slip, completely oblivious to the energy in the room that hummed between Natalie and Colin. Natalie wasn't quite sure how she didn't notice it. It made it hard for

Natalie to breathe. It made the dress feel hot and itchy against her skin even though it was the softest, most delicate fabric ever made.

Colin slipped back down onto the couch with a deep sigh. When he looked up at her again, Natalie knew she wasn't mistaken about any of this. He wanted her. And she wanted him. It was a bad idea, they both knew it, but they couldn't fight it much longer.

She also wanted out of this dress. Right now. Playing bride was a confusing and scary experience. Before Colin or Ruby could say another word, she pulled the veil from her head, leaped down from the pedestal and disappeared behind the curtains into the dressing room as fast as she could.

Six

"I'd like to take you to dinner," Colin said as they walked out of the shop with the gown bagged over his arm. "I'm serious this time. You really bailed me out on this whole dress thing."

It was a lame excuse. It sounded lame to his own ears, but he couldn't do anything about it. There was no way he could look at Natalie, to see her in that dress looking like the most beautiful creature he'd ever set his eyes on, and then let her just get in her car and go home. It no longer mattered if they were incompatible or had no future. The taste of her already lingered on his lips, the heat of her hummed through his veins. He wanted her. End of story.

Natalie stopped and swung her purse strap up onto her shoulder. "Dinner? Not a date?"

This again. You'd think after their kiss, and after the intense moment they'd just shared in the salon, that she wouldn't be so picky about the details. "No, it's not a date, it's a thank-you. I believe that I have yet to meet your stringent qualifications for a date."

Natalie's lips curled into a smile of amusement. He expected her to make an excuse and go home, but instead she nodded. "Dinner sounds great."

Colin opened the door of his truck and hung the gown bag up inside. "How about the Italian place on the corner?"

"That's perfect."

He closed up the truck and they walked down the sidewalk together to the restaurant. Colin had eaten at Moretti's a couple of times and it had always been good. It was rustic Italian cuisine, with a Tuscan feel inside. The walls were a rusty brown with exposed brick, worn wood shelves and tables, warm gold lighting and an entire wall on the far end that was covered in hundreds of wine bottles. It wasn't the fanciest place, but it was a good restaurant for a casual dinner date, or a thank-you dinner as the case was here.

It was a pretty popular place to eat in this area. Typically, Moretti's was super busy, but coming later on a Monday night the restaurant was pretty quiet. There were about a dozen tables with customers when they arrived and no waiting list.

The hostess immediately escorted them to a booth for two near the roaring fireplace. Nashville didn't get very cold in the winter, but with the icy December wind, it was cold enough that the fire would feel amazing after their walk down the street. Colin helped Natalie out of her coat, hanging it on one of the brass hooks mounted to the side of the booth.

The waiter arrived just as they'd settled into their

seats, bringing water and warm bread with olive oil. He offered them the daily menus and left them alone to make their choices. After a bit of deliberation, Natalie chose the angel-hair primavera and Colin, the chicken parmesan. They selected a bottle of cabernet to share and the waiter returned with that immediately.

The first sip immediately warmed Colin's belly and cheeks, reminding him to go slow until he ate some bread. He'd had a quick sandwich around eleven, but he was starving now and wine on an empty stomach might make him say or do something he'd regret, like kissing Natalie again. Or maybe he'd do something he wouldn't regret, but shouldn't do. At the moment, Lily's suggestion that he indulge himself in something casual with Natalie was sounding pretty good. He took a bite of bread as a precaution.

"Well, this is certainly not how I envisioned this evening going," Natalie noted as she tore her own chunk of bread from the loaf.

"It's not bad, is it?"

"No," she admitted. "But when I woke up this morning, I didn't figure I'd be trying on wedding dresses and having dinner with you."

It hadn't been on his radar either, but he was happy with the turn of events. There was something about spending an evening with Natalie that relaxed him after a stressful day. "Did you have plans for tonight that I ruined?"

"Not real plans. I'd anticipated a frozen dinner and a couple chapters of a new book I downloaded."

"I was going to grab takeout and catch up on my DVR. We're an exciting pair. Are you off tomorrow?"

Natalie shrugged, confusing him with her response

to a simple question. "Technically," she clarified. "The chapel is closed on Tuesday and Wednesday, but I usually go in."

"That means you don't get any days off."

"I don't usually work a full day. And I only work half of Sunday to clean up."

Colin shook his head. "You sound as bad as I used to be when I took over Dad's business. I worked eighteen-hour days, seven days a week trying to keep afloat. Is that why you put in so many hours? How's the wedding business?"

If the bill he'd received for the upcoming wedding was any indication, they were doing very well. He'd told her money was no object and she'd believed him. It was well worth it for Lily, but he'd been surprised to see so many digits on the invoice.

"Business is great. That's why it's so hard not to come in. There's always something to do."

"Can't you hire someone to watch the place and answer the phones while you all take time off? Like a receptionist?"

Natalie bit her lip and took a large sip of wine as though she were delaying her response. "I guess we could. Anyways, I'm the only one without a backup, but I'm the only one of us without a life. It's kind of hard to swap out the wedding planner, though. I'm the one with the whole vision of the day and know all the pieces that have to fall into place just perfectly."

"Getting a receptionist isn't the same as getting a backup planner. It just frees you up so you're not answering the phones and filing paperwork all the time. You should look into it. Of course, that would require you not to be such a control freak."

Natalie perked up in her seat. "I am not a control freak."

At that, Colin laughed. "Oh, come on now. Your office is immaculate. You're always stomping around with that headset on, handling every emergency. I'm beginning to think you run a one-stop wedding company because you won't let anyone else do any of it."

She opened her mouth to argue, then stopped. "Maybe I should look into a receptionist," she admitted.

"If you had one, you could spend the next two days with me instead of sitting alone in that lonely office of yours."

Natalie's eyebrow raised in question. "Spend the next two days with you doing what?"

"Working on the house. Helping me decorate. What we discussed last week. I've turned over the reins of the company to my second-in-command to manage our remaining projects through the end of the year so I can focus on what I need to do before the holidays."

"Oh."

That wasn't the enthusiastic response he was hoping for. "Oh, huh? I guess I should sweeten the deal, then. Spending time with me to help your childhood best friend isn't enough incentive."

"Quit it," Natalie chided. "I told you I'd help you with the house. Since I work on weekends, it makes sense to come over tomorrow, you're right. And I will. I was just expecting something else."

"Like what?"

"I don't know…a trip to the Opryland Hotel to look at the Christmas decorations and visit Santa, maybe?"

Opryland! Colin silently cursed and sipped his wine to cover his aggravation. The hotel in central Nashville was practically its own city. They went all out every holiday with massive decorations. They usually built a giant ice village with slides kids could play on. They even hosted the Rockettes' Christmas show. That would've been perfect, but of course he couldn't do it now that she'd brought it up. He refused to be predictable.

There wasn't really time for that, either. When he'd made that impulsive bet, he hadn't given a lot of thought to how much they both worked and how incompatible their schedules were. Between their jobs, working on the house and the wedding, there wasn't much time left to reintroduce Natalie to the holiday magic. He'd find a way, though. He was certain of it.

"I figured it was something related to the bet, although I don't know why you'd bother after that kiss we shared at the cake tasting. I'm not sure the one you'll win will be better than that."

Colin smiled wide. "Are you serious?" he asked.

She looked at him blankly. "Well, yes. It was a pretty good kiss, as kisses go."

"It was an amazing kiss," Colin conceded. "But it won't hold a candle to the kiss I'll get when I win."

Natalie sucked in a ragged breath, her pale skin growing a more peachy-pink tone in the golden candlelight. "I guess as a teenager I never realized how arrogant you were."

"It's not arrogance when it's fact. I intend to make your pulse spike and cheeks flush. I want you to run your fingers through my hair and hold me like you never want to let me go. When I win this bet, I'll kiss you until you're breathless and can't imagine ever kissing anyone else."

He watched Natalie swallow hard and reach a shaky hand out for more wine. He hid away his smile and focused on her so she knew he meant every word.

"Y-you've still g-got to win the bet," she stammered. "I'm pretty sure you've run out of Christmas stuff to mail to the office."

"Don't underestimate me," Colin said. "Those holiday gifts were just to get you in the right mindset." There were a lot of sensory elements to Christmas—the smell of pine and mulling spice, the taste of peppermint and chocolate, the sight of bright lights and colorful poinsettias. "I wanted to…prime the pump, so to speak. When you're ready, that's when I'll move in for the kill."

The waiter arrived with their salads, but Colin had suddenly lost his appetite. He knew what he wanted to taste and it wasn't on the Moretti's menu. A part of him knew it was a mistake to let himself go any further with Natalie, but the other part already knew it was too late. He needed to have her. Knowing nothing would come of it going in, he would be able to compartmentalize it. Just because he rarely had sex for sex's sake didn't mean he couldn't. What they had was a raw, physical attraction, nothing more. Natalie was certainly an enticing incentive to try to start now.

Perhaps if he did, he could focus on something else for a change. He had plenty going on right now, but somehow, Natalie's full bottom lip seemed to occupy all his thoughts.

As they ate, Natalie shifted the conversation to the wedding and his sister, even asking about his business, but he knew neither of them was really interested in talking about that tonight. They just had to get through dinner.

It wasn't until they were halfway through their pasta that she returned to the previous discussion. "I've been thinking," she began. "I think you and I started off on the wrong foot at the engagement party. I'd like us to start over."

"Start over?" He wasn't entirely sure what that meant.

"Yes. When we get done eating, I'm going to once again ask if you'd like to go someplace quiet to talk and catch up. This time, since you're not dating anyone, I hope you'll give a better response."

Was she offering what he thought she was offering? He sincerely hoped so. He finished his wine and busied himself by paying the bill. When the final credit card slip was brought to him, he looked up at Natalie. She was watching him with the sly smile on her face that she'd greeted him with the first time.

"So, Colin," she said softly. "Would you be interested in getting out of here and finding someplace quiet where we could talk and catch up?"

Colin had replayed that moment in his mind several times since the engagement party and now he knew exactly what he wanted to say.

"Your place or mine?"

It turned out to be his place, which was closer. Natalie's heart was pounding as she followed Colin down the hallway and into his kitchen. She'd only been here once before, the night of the engagement party. The house looked quite different tonight. There were no huge catering platters, no skirted tables, no jazz trio. It was just the wide open, modern space he called home.

It actually looked a little plain without everything else. Spartan. Like a model home.

She couldn't help but notice the sharp contrast between it and the warm, welcoming feel of his parents' house. It was about as far as you could get between them. Natalie had no doubt that this was a million-dollar house, but it was far too contemporary in style to suit her.

"May I offer you more wine?" he asked.

"No, thank you," she said, putting her purse down on the white quartz countertop. "I had plenty at dinner." And she had. She was stuffed. Natalie had focused on her food to avoid Colin's heated appraisal and now she regretted it. If she'd fully realized that her fantasies would actually play out after dinner, she would've held back a touch. She didn't exactly feel sexy, full to the gills with pasta, bread and wine.

"May I offer you a tour, then? I'm not sure how much you got to see of the place the other night."

"Not much," Natalie admitted. Since she'd only known the bride and her brother, she hadn't done much socializing. She'd hovered near the bar, people watching most of the evening.

Colin led her out of the sleek kitchen and through the dining room to the two-story open living room with a dramatic marble fireplace that went up to the ceiling. She followed him up the stairs to his loft office, then his bedroom. "This is the best part," he said.

"I bet," Natalie replied with a grin.

"That's not what I meant." He walked past the large bed to a set of French doors. He opened them and stepped out onto a deck.

Natalie went out behind him and stopped short as

she caught a glimpse of the view. They'd driven up a fairly steep hill to get here, she remembered that, but she hadn't realized his house virtually clung to the side of the mountain. While precarious, it offered an amazing view of the city. The lights stretched out as far as the eye could see, competing with the stars that twinkled overhead.

She had a really nice townhouse she liked, but it couldn't hold a candle to this. She could sit out here all night just looking up at the stars and sipping her coffee. Natalie bet it was amazing at sunrise, too.

"So, what do you think?"

Natalie hesitated, trying to find the right words. She turned to Colin, who was leaning against the railing with his arms crossed over his chest. "The deck is amazing."

"What about the rest of the house?"

"It's very nice."

"Nice, huh? You don't like it at all."

Natalie avoided the question by stepping back into the bedroom with him on her heels. "It's a beautiful home, really. The view alone is worth the price you paid for it. The aesthetic is just a little modern for my taste."

Colin nodded. "Me, too. To be honest, Pam picked this place. If I hadn't been so mad about Shane, I probably would've let her keep it."

Natalie stiffened at the mention of his ex-wife and the son who'd turned out not to be his. She still wasn't sure exactly what had happened, but prying seemed rude. Since he brought it up… "Does she ever let you see Shane?"

Colin shook his head once, kind of curt. "No. I think it's better that way though since he's still a baby. If he'd been any older, it would've been harder to help him understand where his daddy was. He's probably forgotten who I am by now."

"I don't know about that," Natalie said, stepping toward him until they were nearly touching. "I know I've never been able to forget about you."

"Is that right?" Colin asked, wrapping his arms around her waist. The pain had faded from his face, replaced only with the light of attraction. "So, did you fantasize about what it would be like to kiss me?"

Natalie smiled. How many nights had she hugged her pillow to her chest and pretended it was Lily's handsome older brother? "An embarrassing number of times," she admitted.

"Did our first kiss live up to those expectations?"

"It did, and then some. Of course, when I was fifteen, I didn't know what was really possible like I do now."

"Oh really?"

"Yes. And now I want more."

Colin didn't hesitate to meet her demand. His mouth met hers, offering her everything she wanted. She ran her fingers through his hair, tugging him closer. Natalie wasn't letting him get away this time. He was all hers tonight. She arched her back, pressing her body against the hard wall of his chest.

He growled against her lips, his hand straying from her waist to glide along her back and hips. He cupped one cheek of her rear through the thin fabric of her skirt, pushing her hips against his until she could feel the firm heat of his desire.

Natalie gasped, pulling from his mouth. "Yeah," she said in a breathy voice. "There's no way I would've imagined a kiss like that."

Pulling back, she reached for the collar of his jacket. She pushed his blazer off his shoulders, letting it fall to the floor. Her palms moved greedily over his broad shoulders and down the front of his chest, touching every inch of the muscles she'd seen in that tight T-shirt. Starting at his collar, she unbuttoned his shirt, exposing the muscles and dark chest chair scattered across them.

Colin stood stiffly as she worked, his hands tightly curled into fists at his sides. When Natalie reached his belt, he sprang into action, grasping her wrists. "That's not really fair, is it?"

"Well," she reasoned, "I've been fantasizing about seeing you naked for years. I think it's only right I shouldn't have to wait any longer."

Colin gathered the hem of her blouse and lifted it slowly over her head. Natalie raised her arms to help him take it off. He cast her shirt onto a nearby chair. "I don't think a few more minutes will kill you."

He focused on her breasts, taking in the sight before covering the satin-clad globes with the palms of his hands. Natalie gasped when he touched her, her nipples hardening and pressing into the restraining fabric. He kneaded her flesh, dipping his head down to taste what spilled over the top of the cups. Colin nipped at her skin, soothing it with the glide of his tongue. Tugging down at her bra, he uncovered her nipples, drawing one, then the next into his mouth.

Natalie groaned, pulling his head closer. The warmth of his mouth on her sensitive flesh built a liquid heat in her core. She wasn't sure how much longer she could take this kind of torture.

"I need you," she gasped. "Please."

In response, Colin sought out the back of her skirt

with his fingers. He unzipped it, letting it slide down over her hips. She stepped out of the skirt and her heels, then let Colin guide her backward through the room until the backs of her legs met with the mattress. She reached behind her, crawling onto the bed.

While Colin watched, she unclasped her bra and tossed it aside, leaving nothing on but her panties. His eyes stayed glued to her as he unfastened his pants and slipped them off with his briefs. He pulled away long enough to retrieve a condom from the bedside stand before he climbed onto the bed.

The heat of his body skimmed over hers. He hovered there, kissing her as one hand roamed across her stomach. It brushed the edge of her panties, slipping beneath to dip his fingers between her thighs. Natalie arched off the bed, gasping before meeting his lips once more. He stroked her again and again, building a tension inside her that she was desperate to release.

Colin waited until she was on the very edge, then he retreated, leaving her panting and dissatisfied. "Just a few more minutes," he reassured her with a teasing grin.

He moved down her body, pulling the panties over her hips and along the length of her legs as he moved. Tossing them aside, he sheathed himself and pressed her thighs apart. He nestled between them and positioned himself perfectly to stroke her core as his hips moved forward and back. He rebuilt the fire in her belly, then, looking her in the eye, shifted his hips and thrust into her.

Natalie cried out, clawing at the blankets beneath her. He started slow, clenching his jaw with restraint, then began moving faster. She drew her legs up, wrapping them around his hips as they flexed, eliciting a low groan deep in Colin's throat.

"Yes," Natalie coaxed as he moved harder and faster inside her.

The release he'd teased at before quickly built up inside her again and this time, she knew she would get what she wanted. She gripped his back, feeling the knot tighten in her belly. "Please," she said.

"As you wish." He thrust hard, grinding his pelvis against her sensitive parts until she screamed out.

"Colin!" she shouted as the tiny fire bursts exploded inside her. Her release pulsated through her whole body, her muscles tightening around him as she shuddered and gasped.

Thrusting again, Colin buried his face in her neck and poured himself into her. "Oh, Natalie," he groaned into her ear.

The sound of her name on his lips sent a shiver down her spine. She wrapped her arms around him as he collapsed against her. She gave him a few minutes to rest and recover before she pushed at his shoulders. "Come on," she said.

"Come where?" He frowned.

"To the shower. You and I are just getting started. I've got fourteen years to make up for."

Seven

Colin was making coffee downstairs the next morning when he heard the heavy footsteps of a sleepy Natalie coming down the stairs. He peeked around the corner in time to see her stumble onto the landing. She'd pulled her messy hair into a ponytail and was wearing her professional office attire, but it was rumpled and definitely looked like a day-two ensemble for her.

He watched as she hesitated at the bottom of the stairs. She looked around nervously, almost like she was searching for an exit route. Was she really trying to sneak out without him seeing her? Yes, there wasn't anything serious between them, but she didn't need to flee the scene of the crime. She started slinking toward the front door, but he wasn't about to let her off so easily.

"Good morning, Natalie," he shouted.

She stiffened at the sound of his voice, and then reluctantly turned and followed the noise toward the kitchen. "Good morning," she said as she rounded the corner.

He loved seeing this unpolished version of her. With her wrinkled clothes, her mussed-up hair and day-old makeup, it was a far cry from the superprofessional and sleek wedding planner at the chapel. It reminded him of just how she'd gotten so messy and made him want to take her back upstairs to see what more damage he could do to her perfect appearance in the bedroom.

From the skittish expression on her face, he doubted he'd get the chance. Last night was likely a one-time event, so he'd have to be content with that. Instead, Colin returned to pouring the coffee he'd made into a mug for each of them. "How do you take your coffee? I have raw sugar, fake sugar, whole milk and hazelnut creamer. Oh, and getting it in a go-cup isn't an option, by the way."

She smiled sheepishly, clearly knowing she'd been caught trying to make a quick getaway. "I promise not to drink on the run. A splash of milk and a spoonful of raw sugar, please."

He nodded and worked on making her the perfect cup. "Would you like to have coffee downstairs or on the deck?"

She looked up at the staircase to the bedroom, which they'd have to pass through to get to the deck. "The kitchen nook is fine," she said, obviously unwilling to risk the pleasurable detour. "I'm sure we missed the best of the sunrise a long time ago."

Colin handed over her mug and followed her to the

table with a plate of toasted English muffins with strawberry jam and butter. He sat down and picked up one muffin, taking a bite with a loud crunch. He finished chewing and let Natalie sip her coffee before he pressed her about her great escape.

"You seem to be in a hurry this morning. What's the rush?"

Natalie swallowed her sip of coffee and set the mug on the kitchen table. "I was hoping you wouldn't notice. It's just that I'm, uh, not used to staying over. I'm sort of a master of the four a.m. vanishing act. I prefer to avoid the awkward morning-after thing."

"You mean coffee and conversation?"

"I suppose," she said with a smile.

"What kept you from leaving last night?" Colin wasn't quite sure what he would've done if he'd woken up and she was gone. He wasn't used to this kind of scenario with a woman. He was a relationship guy, and that usually meant enjoying a nice breakfast after a night together, not cold empty sheets beside him in bed.

"I think it was all the wine we had at dinner on top of the...exercise I got later. When I fell asleep, I slept hard. I didn't so much as move a muscle until I smelled the coffee brewing downstairs."

Colin considered her answer. He tried not to let it hurt his pride that she hadn't stayed because she felt compelled, or even wanted to. "You know, despite what happened last night, we're still friends. I don't want this to change that, so there's no need to run before you turn back into a pumpkin. Do you mind me asking why you feel the need to leave?"

Natalie bit at her lip before nodding. "Like I told you

before, I'm not much on the relationship thing. I like to keep things simple and sweet. Uncomplicated."

What was more complicated than this? Colin couldn't think of anything else. A normal relationship seemed a lot more straightforward. "What does that even mean, Natalie?"

"It means that what we shared last night is all I'm really wanting."

"I get that. And I'm on board with that or I wouldn't have let it go that far last night. I'm just curious as to why you feel this way about guys and relationships in general."

"There's nothing really in it for me after that first night or two because I don't believe in love. I think it's a chemical reaction that's been built up into more. I also don't believe in marriage. I enjoy the occasional companionship, but it's never going to come to any more than that with any man."

Colin listened to her talk, realizing this was worse than he'd thought. It could've just as easily been his ex-wife, Pam, sitting across the table talking to him. Yes, Natalie had said she wasn't the marrying kind, but this was more than just that. She didn't believe in the entire concept. He raised his hand to his head to shake off the déjà vu and the dull throb that had formed at his temple. It was a good thing he knew about her resistance going into this or it could've been a much bigger blow. "A wedding planner that doesn't believe in love or marriage?"

She shrugged. "Just because I don't believe in it doesn't mean that other people can't. I'm organized and I'm detail-oriented. I was made for this kind of work, so why not?"

The whole thing seemed a little preposterous. "So even though you spend all your days helping people get married, you never intend to marry or have a family of your own?"

"No," Natalie said, shaking her head. "You know what I grew up with, Colin. My mother is on the verge of dumping her fourth husband. I've seen too many relationships fall apart to set myself up for that. The heartache, the expense, the legal hassles… I mean, after everything that happened, don't you sometimes wish that you'd never married Pam?"

That wasn't a simple question to answer. He'd spent many nights asking himself the same thing and hadn't quite decided on what he'd choose if he had the power to bend time and do things differently. "Yes and no. Yes, never marrying or even never dating would've been easier on my heart. But more than not getting married, I just wish Shane had been mine. I don't know how long Pam and I would've been able to hold our marriage together, but even if we'd divorced in that case, I'd still have my son. I'd have a piece of the family I want. Now I have nothing but the lost dream of what I could've had. As they say, 'a taste of honey is worse than none at all,' but I wouldn't trade away my time with Shane. The day he was born was the happiest day of my life. And the day I found out he wasn't my son was the worst. I lost my son and I wasn't even allowed to grieve the loss because I never truly had him to begin with."

Natalie frowned into her coffee cup. "That's exactly the kind of heartache I want to stay away from. I can't understand how someone could go through that and be willing to dust themselves off and try again."

"It's called hope. And I can't understand how someone could go through their life alone. Having a family, having children and seeing them grow up is what life is all about."

"Exactly. It's survival of the species, our own biology tricking us into emotional attachments to ensure stability for raising the next generation. Then it fades away and we're left feeling unfulfilled because society has sold us on a romantic ideal that only really exists in movies and books."

Colin could only shake his head. "That's the worst attitude about love I've ever heard."

"I don't force anyone else to subscribe to my ideas. I didn't come up with this overnight, I assure you. I learned the hard way that love is just a biological impulse that people confuse with Hallmark card sentiment. Have you ever noticed that all the fairy tales end when the Prince and Princess get married? That's because the story wouldn't be that exciting if it showed their lives after that. The Prince works too much. The Princess resents that she's constantly picking up his dirty socks and wiping the snotty noses of his children, so she nags at the Prince when he comes home. The Prince has an affair with his secretary. The Princess throws the Prince out of the palace and takes him to court for child support. Not exactly happily ever after."

"Don't ever write children's books," Colin said drily.

"Someone needs to write that book. That way little girls won't grow up believing in something that isn't going to happen. It would save them all a lot of disappointment."

Colin had tasted every inch of Natalie last night and there hadn't been the slightest bitterness, but now, it seemed to seep from every pore. He was frankly stunned by her attitude about love. It was even more deep-seated and angry than Pam's negative ideas. Pam just didn't want the strings of marriage and monogamy. Natalie didn't believe in the entire construct.

"Hopefully you weren't disappointed with last night."

"Of course not. Last night was great, Colin. It was everything that I'd hoped it would be, and more. And by stopping right now, we get to preserve it as the amazing night that it was."

He knew she was right. He could feel it in his bones. But he also couldn't just let this be the end of it. He wouldn't be able to finish dealing with the wedding plans and the house, being so close to her, without being able to touch her again. "What if I wanted another night or two like last night?"

Natalie watched him with a suspicious narrowing of her eyes. "Are you suggesting we have a little holiday fling?"

He shrugged. Colin had never proposed such a thing, so he wasn't entirely sure. "I did bet you that I could put a little jingle in your step. I think the time we spend together would be a lot more fun for us both if we let this attraction between us be what it is. No promise of a future or anything else, and you don't have to dash from the bed like a thief in the night. What do you think?"

"It sounds tempting," she admitted. "I wouldn't mind getting a little more of those toe-curling kisses you promised me. But you have to agree that after the wedding, we part as we started—as old friends. No hard feelings when it's over."

"Okay, it's a deal. I promise not to fall in love with you, Natalie."

"Excellent," she said with a smile before leaning in to plant a soft kiss on his lips. "I don't plan on falling in love with you either."

"So, what do you think?"

Natalie hovered in the doorway of Colin's family home, her mouth agape in shock. It had only been a week since she was in the house, but it had been completely transformed. "Is this the same place?"

Colin smiled. "A lot has happened since you were here. While I have been busy planning Lily's wedding and seducing you, I couldn't just sit around doing nothing all weekend while you were working, you know."

He'd worked magic in Natalie's opinion. A lot of the old furniture and things they didn't want to keep were gone. In their place were new pieces that looked a million times better. There was new paint on the walls, updated light fixtures and window coverings…the place looked better than she ever remembered. "You've worked a miracle."

"I didn't do it alone, I assure you. The Catholic charity came and picked up all the old things we didn't want to keep. I've had contractors in and out all week. We didn't do any major renovations, so it's mostly cosmetic, but I think it turned out nicely."

"Well, what's left for me to do?"

Colin took her hand and led her into the formal dining room. There, in front of the bay window, was a giant Christmas tree. Apparently her plan to distract him with sexual escapades hadn't worked the way she'd thought.

"Colin," she complained, but he raised a hand to silence her.

"Nope. You agreed to go along with the bet. It's not fair if you stonewall my plans. If you're confident enough to win, you're confident enough to decorate a Christmas tree without being affected by the cloying sentimentality of it all."

Natalie sighed. "Okay, fine. We'll trim the tree."

Colin grinned wide. "Great! I got all the decorations down from the attic."

They approached the pile of boxes and plastic totes that were neatly stacked by the wall. He dug around until he found the one with Christmas lights.

"When did you have the time to get a live tree?"

"I went by a tree lot while you went back to your place to shower and change. It took some creative maneuvering to get it into the house, but I was successful. Would you like a drink before we get started?" he asked as he walked into the kitchen.

"Sure. Water would be fine."

"How about some cider?" he called.

Cider? Natalie followed him into the kitchen, where she was assaulted by the scent of warm apple, cinnamon, orange zest and cloves. It was almost exactly like the scented candle she still had sitting on her desk from one of his holiday deliveries. She could hardly believe it, but Colin actually had a small pot of mulled cider simmering on the stove. Sneaky.

She wasn't going to acknowledge it, though. "Some cider would be great," she said. "It's a cold day."

"All right. I'll be right out and we can get started on that tree."

Natalie wandered back into the dining room and stared down the Christmas tree. She hadn't actually been this close to one in a long time. The scent of pine was strong, like the wreath on her door. She'd never had a real tree before. Her mother had always insisted on an artificial tree for convenience and aesthetics. While perfectly shaped and easy to maintain, it was lacking something when compared to a real tree.

The soft melody of music started in another room, growing louder until she could hear Bing Crosby crooning. Before she could say anything, Colin came up to her with a mug of cider and a plate of iced sugar cookies.

"You're kidding, right? Did you seriously bake Christmas cookies?"

"Uh, no," he laughed. "I bought them at a bakery near the tree lot. I didn't have time to do everything."

"You did plenty," she said, trying to ignore Bing's pleas for a white Christmas. "Too much." She sipped gingerly at the hot cider. The taste was amazing, warming her from the inside out. She'd actually never had cider before. It seemed she'd missed out on a lot of the traditional aspects of the holiday by abstaining for so long.

While it was nice, it wasn't going to change how she felt about Christmas in general. Natalie reluctantly set her mug aside and opened the box of Christmas lights. The sooner they got the tree decorated, the sooner she could get out of here.

They fought to untangle multiple strands, wrapping the tree in several sets of multicolored twinkle lights. From there, Colin unpacked boxes of ornaments and handed them one at a time to Natalie to put them on the tree. They were all old and delicate: an assortment of glass balls and Hallmark figurines to mark various family milestones.

"Baby's First Christmas," Natalie read aloud. It was a silver rattle with the year engraved and a festive bow tied around it. "Is this yours?"

Colin nodded. "Yep. My mom always bought a few ornaments each year. This one," he said, holding up Santa in a boat with a fishing pole, "was from the year we went camping and I caught my first fish."

Natalie examined the ornament before adding it to the tree with the others. "That's a sweet tradition."

"There are a lot of memories in these boxes," Colin said. "Good and bad." He unwrapped another ornament with a picture of his parents set between a pair of pewter angel wings.

When he handed it to Natalie, she realized it was a memorial ornament and the picture was one taken right before their accident. It seemed an odd thing to put on the Christmas tree. Why would he decorate with bad memories?

"Put it near the front," Colin instructed. "I always want our parents to be a part of our Christmas celebration."

Natalie gave the ornament a place of honor, feeling herself get a little teary as she looked at the two of them smiling, with no idea what was ahead for them and their children. "I miss them," she said.

Colin nodded. "Me, too." He took a bite of one of the iced snowman cookies. "Mom's were better," he said.

That was true. Mrs. Russell had made excellent cookies. But as much as Natalie didn't like the holidays, she didn't want to bring down the evening Colin planned with sad thoughts. "Do we have many more ornaments?"

The sad look on Colin's face disappeared as he focused on the task of digging through the box. "Just one more." He handed over a crystal dove. "Now we just need some sparkle."

Together, they rolled out the red satin tree skirt with the gold-embroidered poinsettias on it, then they finished off the last decorating touches. Colin climbed onto a ladder to put the gold star on the top of the tree while Natalie wrapped some garland around the branches.

"Okay, I think that's it," Colin said as he climbed down from the ladder and stepped back to admire their handiwork. "Let's turn out the lights and see how it looks."

Natalie watched him walk to the wall and turn out the overhead chandelier for the room. She gasped at the sight of the tree as it glowed in front of the window. The red, green, blue and yellow lights shimmered against the walls and reflected off the glass and tinsel of the tree.

Colin came up behind her and wrapped his arms around her waist. She snuggled into him, feeling herself get sucked into the moment. The tree, the music, the scents of the holidays and Colin's strong embrace… it all came together to create a mood that stirred long-suppressed emotions inside her.

"I think we did a good job," Colin whispered near her ear.

"We did a great job," she countered, earning a kiss on the sensitive skin below her earlobe. It sent a shiver through her body with goose bumps rising up across her flesh.

"Are you cold?" he asked. "I can turn on the gas fireplace and we can drink our cider there. Soak in the ambience."

"Sure," Natalie said. She picked up her cider and the plate of cookies and followed Colin into the living room. Natalie noticed that above the fireplace were a pair of stockings with both Lily's and Frankie's names embroidered on them. There was pine garland with lights draped across the mantel with tall red pillar candles and silk poinsettias. It was perfect.

With the flip of a switch, the fireplace roared to life. Colin settled down on the love seat and Natalie snuggled up beside him. She kicked off her shoes and pulled her knees up to curl against him. It was soothing to lie there with his arm around her, his heartbeat and the Christmas carols combining to create a soundtrack for the evening.

It had been a long time since Natalie had a moment like this. She didn't limit herself to one-night stands, but her relationships had focused more on the physical even if they lasted a few weeks. She hadn't realized how much she missed the comfort of being held. How peaceful it felt to sit with someone and just be together, even without conversation.

Sitting still was a luxury for Natalie. Once they had opened the chapel there was always something to be done, and she liked it that way. Now she was starting to wonder if she liked it that way because it filled the holes and distracted her from what she was missing in her life. Companionship. Partnership. Colin hadn't convinced her to love Christmas again, but he had opened her eyes to what she'd been missing. She could use more time like this to just live life.

Unfortunately, time like this with a man like Colin came with strings. It had only been a few short hours since they'd agreed to a casual fling, but in her heart, Natalie still worried.

While the decisive and successful owner of Russell Landscaping was driven and in control of his large company, the Colin she'd always known was also sentimental and thoughtful on the inside. The business success and the money that came with it were nice, but she could tell that he'd done all that to honor his father's memory. And more than anything, he wanted his own family, and had since he lost his parents. No little fling would change that.

She liked Colin a lot, but even her teenage infatuation couldn't turn it into more than that. More than that didn't exist in her mind. She could feel her hormones raging and her thoughts kept circling back to Colin whether she was with him or not, but that wasn't love. That was biology ensuring they would continue to mate until she conceived. He might be attracted to her now, but she would never be the wife and mother he envisioned sitting around the Christmas tree with their children. She just wasn't built for that.

Natalie knew she had to enjoy her time with Colin, then make sure it came to a swift end before either of them got attached to the idea of the two of them. She was certain that their individual visions of "together" would be radically different.

"That wasn't so bad, was it?" Colin asked.

The question jerked Natalie from her thoughts and brought her back to the here and now, wrapped in Colin's arms. "It wasn't," she admitted. "I have to say that was the most pleasant tree decorating experience I've had in ten years."

"Natalie, have you even decorated a Christmas tree in ten years?"

Of course he'd ask that. "Nope. I appreciate all your efforts, but even if it had been a miserable night, it still would've been the best. So sorry, but you haven't won the bet yet."

Eight

Tomorrow night, Natalie's cell phone screen had read on Wednesday.

Colin followed it up with another text. *You and I are going on a date. Per your requirements, you will wear a pretty dress and I will take you someplace nice. I will pick you up at seven.*

She ignored the warning bells in her head that insisted a real date fell outside their casual agreement. While going on a date with Colin had the potential to move them forward in a relationship with nowhere to go, it also might do nothing other than provide them both with a nice evening together. She tried not to read too much into it.

Natalie made a point of not staying at work too late on Thursday so she could get home and get ready for their date. She ignored the pointed and curious glare of Gretchen when she announced that she was leaving early. She would deal with that later.

Back at her townhouse, she pored through her closet looking for just the right dress. She settled on a gray-and-silver lace cocktail dress. It was fitted with a low-plunging scalloped V-neckline that enhanced what small bit of cleavage she had. It also had shimmering silver bands that wrapped around the waist, making her boyish figure appear more seductively hourglass-shaped.

Once that was decided, she spent almost a half hour flatironing her hair. She wore it in a ponytail most every day. At work, she liked it off her face, but tonight, she wanted it down and perfect.

The doorbell rang exactly at seven and Natalie tried not to rush toward the door. She took her time, picking up her silver clutch on the way.

"Hello there," Natalie said as she opened the door.

Colin didn't respond immediately. His gaze raked over her body as he struggled to take it all in. Finally, he looked at her and smiled. "I like going on dates with you, pretty dress and all."

She preened a little, taking a spin to show off how good her butt looked in the dress before pulling her black wool dress coat from the closet. "I made a big deal of tonight's requirements so I wanted to hold up my end of the bargain."

Colin held out her jacket to help her into it. "You certainly have. You look amazing tonight."

"Thank you."

"Your chariot awaits," Colin said, gesturing toward a silver Lexus Coupe in the driveway.

"Where's the truck?" she asked.

"I didn't think you'd feel like climbing up into it when you're dressed up. Besides, this car matches your dress. It's fate."

He helped her into the car and they drove through town, bypassing some of the usual date spots and heading toward one of the high-end outdoor shopping plazas in Nashville. "Where are we going?" she asked as they pulled into the crowded parking lot. She made a point of avoiding any major shopping areas in December. She was guaranteed to run into Christmas music, decorations and grumpy people fighting their way through their chore lists.

"You'll see," Colin replied, ignoring her squirming in the seat beside him.

"Is this part of the Christmas bet? Telling me you're taking me on a date, letting me get all dressed up and then taking me to see Santa at the mall is cruel. I can assure you it won't fill me with Christmas spirit. More than likely, it will fill me with impatience and a hint of rage. These heels are pretty and expensive, but I'm not above throwing them at someone."

Colin just laughed at her and pulled up to the valet stand at the curb. "Keep your shoes on. I doubt you'll have need to use them as a weapon. I didn't bring you here for the holiday chaos. I brought you here for the best steak and seafood in Nashville."

"Oh," she said quietly. There *were* some nice restaurants here; it was just hard to think about going to them in mid-December. Natalie waited until Colin opened her door and helped her out of the car. "What's that under your arm?" she asked as they made their way through the maze of shops.

Colin looked down at the neatly wrapped package

beneath his arm and shrugged. "It's just a little something."

Natalie wrinkled her nose in a touch of irritation. She hated surprises, hated not knowing every detail of what was going on in any given situation. Being a wedding planner allowed her to legitimately be a control freak. She wanted to press the issue with him but let the subject go since they were approaching the heavy oak doors of the restaurant. A man opened one for them, welcoming them inside the dark and romantic steakhouse. They checked in and were taken back to a private booth away from the main foot traffic of the restaurant.

They ordered their food and a bottle of wine, settling in for a long, leisurely dining experience. "So, now will you tell me what's in the box?"

Colin picked up the shiny silver package. "You mean this box?" he taunted.

"Yes. That's the one."

"Not right now. I have something else to discuss."

Natalie's eyebrow went up. "You do, do you?"

"Yes. I was wondering what you're doing Sunday evening."

Natalie wished she had her tablet with her. "Sunday morning, we clean and break down from Saturday's wedding. I don't think I have plans that night, aside from kicking off my shoes and relaxing for the first time in three days."

"That doesn't sound like it's any fun. I think you should consider coming with me to a Christmas party."

"Oh no," Natalie said, shaking her hand dismissively. "That's okay. I'm not really comfortable at that kind of thing."

"What's there to be uncomfortable about? We'll eat,

drink and mingle. Aside from the reason for the party, you might even forget it's a holiday gathering."

"Yes, but I won't know anyone there. I'm awful at small talk."

"Actually, you'll know everyone. It's Amelia Dixon's party."

"Amelia?" Natalie frowned. "My friend Amelia invited *you* to a Christmas party?"

Colin took a sip of his wine and nodded. "She did. Why are you so surprised? Did she not invite you?"

Honestly, Natalie wasn't sure. She didn't really pay much attention to her mail this time of year if it didn't look like an important bill of some kind. A few folks, Amelia included, always seemed to send her a Christmas card despite her disinterest. If she'd gotten an invite, it was probably in her trash can.

"I typically don't attend Amelia's Christmas party. I'm more curious as to how you got invited. You don't even know her."

"I know her well enough for a little Christmas gathering when I'm dating her close friend."

"Are we dating?" Natalie asked.

"And more importantly," he continued, ignoring her question, "I think she understands you better than you'd like to think. I get the feeling she invited me to make sure you showed up this time."

"I wouldn't be surprised." Amelia had proved in the past that she was a scheming traitor when it came to men. She'd lured Bree to a bar to see Ian after they broke up. Natalie had no doubt she would stoop to similar levels to push her and Colin together *and* get her to come to her annual Christmas soirée. "Despite how much she pesters me, she knows I won't come."

"Well this year, I think you should make an exception and go. With me."

She could feel her defenses weakening. It all sounded nice, and she couldn't wait to see what kind of party Amelia could throw in their big new house with all that entertaining space. But she wished it didn't have to be a Christmas party. The last Christmas party she went to was for kids. Santa was there handing out little presents to all the children, they ate cupcakes and then they made reindeer out of clothespins. She was pretty certain that wasn't what they'd be doing at Amelia and Tyler's. What did adults even do at Christmas parties? "I don't know, Colin."

"It's settled, you're coming." Colin picked up his phone and RSVP'd to Amelia while they were sitting there. Natalie opened her mouth to argue, but it was too late. There was no getting out of it now. Amelia would insist and there would be no squirming.

"Why do you hate me?" Natalie asked as he put his phone away.

"I don't hate you. I like you. A lot. That's why I'm so determined to make the most of our short time together. It also doesn't hurt that it might help me win that kiss." His hazel eyes focused on her across the table, making her blood heat in her veins.

Natalie sighed, trying to dismiss her instant reaction to him. "I've kissed you twenty times. What's so important about *that* kiss?"

"It's The One. The most important kiss of all. Nothing can compare to it, I assure you. But I'll make you a deal," he offered.

"A deal? Does it allow me to skip the Christmas

party? I'll gladly spend that whole night naked in your bed if you'll let me skip the stupid party."

Colin's lips curled up in a smile that dashed her hopes of that negotiation. "While that sounds incredibly tempting, no. You're going to that party with me. But, if you promise to come and not give me grief about it the entire time, I'll let you open this box." He picked up the silver-wrapped box with the snowflake hologram bow and shook it tantalizingly at her.

Considering she was pretty much stuck going to the party anyway, she might as well agree and finally soothe her curiosity about that package. "Okay," Natalie conceded. "I will go with you to the party, and I will not bellyache about it."

"Excellent. Here you go."

Natalie took the box from Colin's hand, shaking it to listen for any telltale clues. No such luck. She'd just have to open it. Peeling away at a corner, she pulled back the wrapping to expose a white gift box. Lifting the lid, she found a Swarovski-crystal-covered case for her tablet.

This wasn't some cheap knockoff they sold at the flea markets. Natalie had done enough weddings to recognize real Swarovski crystal when she saw it. She'd seen covers like these in the hands of Paris Hilton and other celebrities. Out of curiosity, she'd looked it up online once and found far too many zeroes at the end to even consider it. It was impossibly sparkly, each crystal catching the flickering candlelight of the restaurant, and it twinkled like thousands of diamonds in her hands. It cast a reflection on the ceiling like stars overhead.

"Do you like it?" Colin asked.

"Yes, I love it. I've always wanted one, but I don't

think I ever told anyone that. What made you think to buy me something like this?"

"Well," Colin explained, "whenever I see you at the chapel, you've got your iPad in your hands. It's like a third arm you can't live without. It seemed a little boring though. I thought a girl that drove a little red sports car might like a little bling in her life. Besides, jewelry seemed…predictable."

Natalie shook her head. "I'm pretty certain that a fling doesn't call for gifts, much less jewelry. This is too much, really. What is this for?"

"It's your Christmas present. I thought you could make good use of it at your upcoming weddings so I wanted to give it to you early. Besides, we're not supposed to make it to Christmas, so I thought if I was going to give you something, the sooner the better."

"It's perfect," Natalie said. Even as she ran her fingertips over the shining stones, she felt guilty. Not just because he'd bought her a gift, but because Colin had given it to her early because she was too flaky to stick with a relationship for two more weeks. She shouldn't feel bad, though. They'd agreed to the arrangement. It had even been his suggestion, and yet she found herself already dreading this coming to an end. "But you shouldn't have done it. It's too much money."

Colin only shrugged at her complaints. "What is the point of earning all this money if I don't do anything with it? I wanted to buy you something and this is what I came up with. End of discussion."

"I haven't gotten you anything," she argued. And she hadn't. She hadn't bought a Christmas gift in years and she was adamant about not receiving one. Every year she had to remind people she was on the naughty list, so no gifts. It had worked so far. Then Colin came in and started busting down every wall she had, one at a time. Soon, if she wasn't careful, she'd be completely exposed.

Colin reached across the table and took her hand. "You've given me plenty without you even knowing it. The last year has been really hard for me with the divorce and everything else. For the first time since I found out about Shane, I'm excited for what each day holds. That's all because of you."

"That may have been the most amazing bread pudding I've ever had," Natalie said as they stepped out of the restaurant and back into the mingling flow of holiday shoppers.

"It was excellent, I have to admit." He wasn't entirely sure where he wanted to take Natalie next, but he knew he didn't want to rush home. Not because he didn't want to make love to her again, but because he wanted her to take in some of the holiday ambience. This was a shopping center in December, but it wasn't the day-after-Thanksgiving crush. There was rarely a riot over a sale at the Louis Vuitton.

He also wanted to simply spend time with Natalie. He'd meant what he said in the restaurant earlier. For the past year, he'd been going through the motions, trying to figure out what his life was supposed to be like now that he wasn't a husband or a father any longer. It had been easy to focus on work, to center all this attention on expanding Russell Landscaping into Chattanooga and Knoxville.

It wasn't until his sister announced her engagement that he'd snapped out of his fog. Pam may not have been the right woman for him, but there was someone out there who could make him happy. He'd started dating again, unsuccessfully, but he was out there. And then he'd spied Natalie at the engagement party and his heart had nearly stilled in his chest from the shock of how beautiful she'd become.

How had the quiet teenager with the dark braid, the braces and the always-serious expression grown up into such a beauty? The timing was terrible, but Colin had known that he would do whatever he had to do to have Natalie in his life again.

Of course, at the time, Colin hadn't known about her pessimistic stance on love and marriage. That had been like a dousing of ice water. It was cruel for the universe to bring him into contact with such a smart, beautiful, talented woman, then make it impossible for them to have any kind of chance of being together. She even hated Christmas. That was a smack in the face of everything he held dear.

Their night together after the bridal shop had just been a chance to release the unbearable pressure building up. He had been dismayed to wake the next morning and find he wanted Natalie more than ever. Continuing to see each other casually until the wedding was a good idea in theory, but it was prolonging the torture in practice. This date, this night together, would probably do more harm than good in the end. But he couldn't stop himself.

Colin knew he was playing with fire. He hadn't gone into this thinking any of it would happen the way it had, or that he could somehow change Natalie's mind. At least about love and marriage. His determination to help her find her Christmas spirit had made slow progress, but progress nonetheless. He could already see cracks in that facade after only a week of trying.

He could see a similar weakness when she was around him. Her mouth was saying one thing while her body was saying another. When she'd stepped out in that wedding gown, it was like nothing existed but her. As much as she built up her theories about biology interfering in relationships, he could tell she was comfortable around him. Happy. Passionate. If they could both be convinced to take whatever this was beyond the wedding, there would be more between them than just sex.

But would what she was willing to give him be enough to make him happy? Companionship and passion seemed nice, but without love in the mix, it would grow tired, or worse, she might stray, like Pam. Without the commitment of love and marriage, there was no glue to hold two people together. It didn't matter how alluring or wonderful Natalie seemed, she would never be the woman he wanted and needed. But for now, for tonight, none of that mattered. They'd had a nice dinner and he had a bet to win. Reaching out, he took her hand. "How about a stroll to walk some of that dinner off?" he asked.

"I probably need to."

They walked together through the outdoor mall, passing a trio of musicians playing Christmas carols. Farther up ahead, Colin could spy the giant Christmas tree that the mayor had lit the week before. The whole place was decorated. There were white twinkle lights in all the bushes and wrapped around each light post. Near the fountain was a fifteen-foot gold reindeer with a wreath of holly and a cluster of oversize ornaments around his neck.

"The lights are pretty," Natalie admitted as they neared the big tree. "It reminds me of the tree in Rockefeller Center."

"Now why would a Grinch go see the tree in New York?" he asked.

"I was there on business," she insisted. "I went down to see the ice skaters and there it was. It's pretty hard to miss."

They approached the black wrought iron railing that surrounded and protected the tree. It, too, was wrapped in lighted garland and big velvet bows. Colin rested his elbows on the railing and looked up at the big tree. "I think our tree is nicer."

Natalie cozied up beside him and studied the tree more closely. "I think you're right. This tree is kind of impersonal. Ours had a special something."

"Maybe we need hot cider," he suggested.

"No," Natalie groaned, pushing away from the railing. "There is no room left in me for anything, even hot cider."

She reached for his hand and he took hers as they started back to the other end of the shopping center where they'd left his car.

"Thank you for bringing me here tonight," she said. "I've never seen this place decorated for the holidays. It's pretty. And not as crowded and chaotic as I was expecting it to be."

"I'm glad you think so," Colin said with a chuckle. "If you'd have been miserable, it could've set me back days."

"No," Natalie said, coming to a stop. "It's perfect. A great first date, I have to say."

"It's not over yet." As they paused, Colin noticed a decorative sprig of mistletoe hanging from a wire overhead. He couldn't have planned this better if he'd tried. "Uh-oh," he said.

Natalie's eyes grew wide. "What? What's wrong?"

Colin pointed up and Natalie's gaze followed. He took a step closer to her, wrapping his arms around her waist. "That's mistletoe up there. I guess I'm going to have to kiss you."

"Sounds like a hardship," she said. "Christmas is such a burdensome holiday. Shop, eat, decorate, make out… I don't know how you people stand it every year with all these demands on your time."

"Am I wrong or does it sound like you're coming around to Team Christmas?"

Natalie wrapped her arms around his neck and entwined her fingers at his collar. "I wouldn't say I'm that far gone yet. A lot hinges on this kiss, though. I've never been kissed under the mistletoe, so I can't understate how critical this moment is to you potentially winning this bet."

"No pressure," Colin said with a smile. Dipping his head, he pressed his lips to hers. Her mouth was soft and yielding to him. She tasted like the buttery bourbon sauce from the bread pudding and the coffee they'd finished their meal with. He felt her melt into him, his fingertips pressing greedily into her supple curves.

Every time he kissed Natalie, it was like kissing her for the first time. There was a nervous excitement in his chest, tempered by a fierce need in his gut. Combined, it urged him to touch, taste and revel in every sweet inch of her.

As they pulled apart, Colin felt the cold kiss of ice against his skin. Opening his eyes, he saw a flurry of snowflakes falling around them. "It's snowing!" he said in surprise. Nashville did get cold weather, but snow was an unusual and exciting event. "How's that for your first kiss under the mistletoe? I kiss you and it starts to snow."

"Wow, it really is snowing." Natalie took a step back, tipping her face up to the sky. She held out her arms, letting the snowflakes blanket her dark hair and speckle her black coat. She spun around, grinning, until she fell, dizzy, back into Colin's arms. "I guess I haven't been paying enough attention to the weatherman," she admitted when she opened her eyes.

"I'm not sure snow was in the forecast. It must be a little Christmas magic at work." Colin looked around as the other shoppers quickly made their way back to their cars. Not everyone appreciated the shift in the weather. In the South, snow typically ended up turning icy and the roads would get bad pretty quickly. They all had to make an emergency run to the grocery store for milk, bread and toilet paper in case they lost power.

He wasn't worried about any of that. Colin just wanted to be right here, right now, with a flushed and carefree Natalie in his arms. She'd worn her hair down tonight for the first time and it looked like dark silk falling over her shoulders and down her back. The cold had made her cheeks and the tip of her nose pink, accentuating the pale porcelain of her complexion.

But most enticing of all was the light of happiness in her eyes. It was the authentic smile he'd been so desperate to lure out of her. The combination threatened to knock the wind out of him every time he looked at her.

"When I picked you up for our date tonight, I didn't think you could get more beautiful," he admitted. Colin brushed a snowflake from her cheek. "I was wrong. Right this moment, you are the most beautiful woman I've ever laid eyes on."

Natalie tried to avoid his gaze and ignore his compliment. He wasn't sure why she was so uncomfortable hearing the truth. She was beautiful and she needed to believe it.

Instead, with a dismissive shake of her head, she said, "Flattery won't help you win the bet, Colin."

"I'm not trying to win a bet," he said, surprising even himself. "I'm trying to win you."

Nine

"You're here!" Amelia nearly shrieked when she spied Natalie and Colin come through the front door of the sprawling mansion in Belle Meade she and Tyler had bought earlier that year. "I didn't believe it when he said you'd agreed to come."

"It's not a big deal," Natalie muttered as she slipped out of her jacket. "You just saw me this morning."

Amelia took both their coats to hang them in the hall closet. "It's not about seeing you, it's about seeing you at my Christmas party. That's a pretty big deal, considering you've never bothered to come before."

"You always held it at your cramped apartment before," Natalie argued, although Colin doubted that the setting had anything to do with it.

"Whatever," Amelia said dismissively. "The important thing is that both of you are here. Come in. Everyone is in the kitchen, of course. Thousands of square feet and everyone congregates there."

Colin took Natalie's hand and led her away from the nearest exit into the house. It was a massive home, large even by his standards, though it looked as if Amelia and her husband were still trying to accumulate enough furniture to fill it up. They had the place beautifully decorated for the holidays, though. A cluster of multiple-sized Christmas trees with lights sat by the front window like a small indoor forest. A decorated tree that had to be at least fourteen feet tall stood in the two-story family room. Any smaller and it would've been dwarfed by the grand size of the house. The banisters were wrapped with garland and ribbon. There was even holiday music playing in the background. Colin was pleased to drag Natalie to a proper holiday gathering.

"Everyone, this is another of my friends and coworkers, Natalie, and her date, Colin. He owns Russell Landscaping."

A few welcomes and hellos sounded from the crowd of about twenty-five people milling through the kitchen, dining room and keeping room area. He recognized a few of them—the wedding photographer, Bree, and Gretchen, the decorator. Bree was hanging on the arm of a dark-headed guy in a black cashmere sweater. Gretchen was alone despite the huge diamond on her finger. He wasn't sure what that was about.

"What would you like to drink?" Amelia asked, rattling off a long list of options.

"I also have a nice microbrew from a place downtown," Tyler offered, holding up a chilled bottle he pulled from the refrigerator.

"Perfect," Colin said, taking it from his hand. Natalie opted for a white wine that Amelia poured for her.

"Help yourself to something to eat. There's plenty, of course," Amelia said, gesturing to the grand buffet table along the wall.

Plenty was an understatement. The caterer in her had gone wild. He and Natalie perused the table, taking in all their options. There were chafing dishes with hot hors d'oeuvres like barbecued meatballs, chicken wings and fried vegetable eggrolls, platters of cold cheeses, finger sandwiches, crudités, dips and crackers, and more desserts than he could identify.

"She's gone overboard," Natalie said. "This is enough to feed a hundred wedding guests. She's just no good at cooking for small numbers. You'd think being pregnant would slow her down, but she's like a machine in the kitchen."

After surveying everything, they each made a plate and moved over to a sitting area with a low coffee table. They ate and chatted with folks as they milled around. Eventually Gretchen approached with her own plate and sat down with them.

"I'm sorry Julian couldn't be here with you tonight," Natalie said.

Gretchen just smiled and shrugged. "It's okay. He's almost done refilming some scenes the director wanted to change and then he'll be home. We'll have a great first Christmas together even though he missed this."

"Your fiancé is in the movie business?" Colin asked.

Gretchen nodded. "Yes, he's an actor. You've probably heard of him. Julian Cooper?"

Colin hesitated midbite. "Really?"

"I know, right?" Gretchen said. "Not who you'd expect me to be with."

"That's not what I meant," he countered. "I'm sure he's very lucky to have you. I've just never met anyone famous before. Feels odd to be one degree of separation from an action hero."

Gretchen smiled, obviously bolstered by his compliment. "You're also officially four degrees from Kevin Bacon."

Colin laughed and lifted his drink to take another sip.

"Excuse me, did I hear Amelia say you own Russell Landscaping?" the man beside him asked.

Colin turned his attention to his right. "Yes." He held out his hand to shake with the man, turning on his bright, businessman charm. "I'm Colin Russell."

"I'm in the construction business with Bree's father," he explained. "I'd love to talk to you about landscaping at our latest project. We're breaking ground on an apartment complex in the spring and looking for a company to handle that for us."

On cue, Colin pulled out his wallet and handed the man his business card. He lost himself in work discussions, realizing after about ten minutes that both Natalie and Gretchen had disappeared.

"Give me a call and we'll set something up," Colin concluded. "I'm going to hunt down my date."

Getting up, Colin carried his empty plate into the kitchen and got a fresh drink. Amelia was buzzing around with Bree helping her, but the others weren't in there. He wandered back into the living room toward the entry hall. Maybe they'd gone to the restroom as a pair, the way women tended to do.

He'd almost reached the entry when he heard Gretchen's voice. Still cloaked in the dark shadows of the room lit only with Christmas lights, he stopped and listened.

"All right, spill," Gretchen said.

Colin heard a hushing sound and some footsteps across the tile floor of the hallway. "Are you crazy?" Natalie asked in a harsh whisper. "Someone is going to hear you. What if Colin heard you?"

"Come on, Natalie. He's all tied up in talk about shrubs and mulch. It's perfectly safe. Tell me the truth. Bree and I have twenty bucks wagered on your answer."

"You're betting on my love life?"

Colin chuckled at Natalie's outrage. He liked her friends.

"Not exactly. We're betting on your emotional depth. That's probably worse. See, Bree thinks you're a shallow pool and believes your big talk when you go on about love not being real and blah, blah."

"And you?" Natalie asked.

"I think you've changed since you met Colin. You've bebopped around the office for the last week like you're on cloud nine. You've been texting him all the time. You haven't been as cranky. You were even humming a Christmas carol this morning."

"So, I'm in a good mood."

"Natalie, you even forgot about a bridal appointment on your calendar tomorrow morning. Your mind isn't on your work, and I think it's because you've realized you were wrong."

Colin held his breath. He was curious to hear what Natalie was going to say but worried he was going to get caught listening in. He leaned against the wall, casually sipping his beer as though he were just waiting for Natalie's return. Even then, he strained to catch the conversation over the holiday music.

"Wrong about what?"

"Wrong about love. You are in love with Colin. Admit it."

Colin's eyes widened. Would his skeptical Natalie really say such a thing? If she did, it could change everything.

"I am not," she insisted, but her voice wasn't very convincing.

Gretchen seemed to agree. "That's a load of crap. I get that you haven't been in love before, and until recently, neither had I. But when it hits you, you know it. And it's not biology or hormones or anything else. It's love. And you, sister, have fallen into it."

"I don't know, Gretchen. This is all new to me. I'm not sure I would call this love."

"Is he the first thing you think about in the morning and the last thing you think of at night? Is he the person you can't wait to share good news with? Does your busy workday suddenly drag on for hours when you know you'll get to see him that night?"

"Yes. Yes, yes and yes," Natalie said almost groaning. "What am I going to do?"

That wasn't exactly the reaction Colin was hoping for when a woman declared her love for him. Yes, she loved him, but she was miserable about it. Considering this was skeptical Natalie, he supposed that shouldn't surprise him. She'd go down kicking and screaming.

"Just go with it," Gretchen encouraged. "Love is awesome."

That was enough for him. Colin was about to cut it too close if he loitered here any longer. He scooted silently across the plush living room carpeting toward the kitchen to get something to nibble on and wait for Natalie's return. While he tried to look calm on the outside, he was anything but.

Could it be true? Was Natalie really in love with him? It had only been a few short weeks, but they'd technically known each other for years. Stranger things had happened. If he was honest with himself, he was having feelings for her as well. He could've answered yes to all of Gretchen's questions. Was that love? He was as clueless as Natalie there. He'd loved his parents, his son, but his attempts to fall in love with a woman had failed.

He felt more deeply for Natalie than he had for any other woman, even Pam. He was mature enough to admit that whole marriage had been about Shane, not about love.

Love. Was that what this was?

It could be. It felt different, somehow. Despite everything going on in his life, he was preoccupied with the brunette who had challenged him at every turn. She was like quicksand, drawing him in deeper the more he struggled against her. Colin had gone into this fling keeping his heart in check, or at least he'd tried to. Natalie wasn't the kind of woman he could settle down with and he knew that. But after spending time with her, he knew this couldn't be just a fling, either. He wanted more, and if Natalie was honest with herself, he was certain she wanted more, too. It was just a matter of convincing her not to run the moment her emotions got too serious or complicated. She might believe in love now, but he got the feeling that getting Natalie to believe in the beauty and power of a good marriage would be the challenge of a lifetime.

Colin popped a chocolate mint petit four into his mouth, looking up in time to see Natalie and Gretchen stroll back into the room. Natalie looked a little pale from their revealing discussion, her ashen color enhanced by her black dress.

No, Natalie might be in love with him, but she was anything but happy about it.

"You've been awfully quiet tonight," Colin said as they pulled into her driveway. "You've hardly said a thing since we left Amelia and Tyler's place."

Natalie shrugged it off, although she felt anything but cavalier about the thoughts racing through her head. "I'm just a little distracted tonight," she said. To soothe his concerns, she leaned in and kissed him. "I'm sorry. Would you like to come in?"

"I would," he said with a smile.

They got out of the car and went into her townhouse. Natalie didn't normally feel self-conscious about her place, but after being at Colin's and Amelia's, her little two-story home felt a bit shabby. Or maybe she was just an emotional live wire after everything that happened at the party.

"Nice place," Colin said as he pulled the door shut behind him.

"Thanks. It's nothing fancy, but it suits me." She led him through the ground floor, absentmindedly prattling on about different features. Mentally, she was freaking out, and had been since Gretchen cornered her at the party. Yes, she'd been quiet. She'd been analyzing every moment of the past two weeks. Was it possible that *she* was the one to break their casual arrangement and fall in love with Colin? Surely it hadn't been long enough for something like that to happen. They'd only been out a few times together.

Then again, Gretchen and Julian fell in love in a week. Bree and Ian fell in love again over a long weekend trapped in a cabin. Amelia had given Tyler thirty days to fall in love and they hadn't needed that long.

So it *was* possible. But was it smart?

Her brain told her no. Love equals heartache. But she couldn't stop herself from sinking further into the warm sensation of love. Colin made it so easy by being everything she never knew she always wanted. She wished he hadn't been so charming and thoughtful so it would be easier to fight.

But even if she *was* in love, it didn't change anything. It didn't mean she wanted to get married. Marriages seemed to ruin good relationships. Maybe it was marriage, not love, that was the real problem.

As Natalie turned to look at him, she realized he had an expectant expression on his face. "What?" she asked.

"I just complimented you on your large collection of classic country vinyl albums," he said, gesturing toward the shelf with her stereo and turntable.

Natalie glanced over at her albums and nodded. "My father bought a lot of them for me," she said. "We used to go to thrift stores looking for old records on Saturday afternoons."

"I mentioned it twice before you heard a word I said." Colin chuckled softly. "You're on another planet tonight, aren't you?"

"I am. I'm sorry." Natalie racked her brain for a way to distract him. She certainly wasn't going to tell him how she was feeling. Running her gaze over his sharply tailored suit, she decided to fall back on her earlier distraction tactic—seduction. She wrapped her arms around his waist and looked up at him. “Have I told you just how handsome you look tonight?”

He smiled, all traces of concern disappearing as he looked down at her adoringly. “Not in the last hour or so.”

“Well, you do,” she said, slipping her hands into his back pockets to grab two solid handfuls of him. “It’s enough to make a girl want to throw the bet so she can experience that amazing kiss you’ve promised.”

Colin shook his head. “There’s no throwing the bet. You either shed your humbug ways or you don’t. Either way, I’m not giving up until you’ve been converted. I don’t care how long it takes.”

“Even after I’ve won?” she asked.

“You bet. I think Christmas in Buenos Aires will be lovely, and I’ll see to it that it is.”

Natalie laughed. “You’re inviting yourself to my vacation prize? I don’t recall asking for company.”

“I don’t recall asking permission. I am paying for the trip, after all.”

Natalie twisted her lips in thought. She was both thrilled and terrified by the idea of Colin still being in her life a year from now. She was so confused about all of this, she didn’t know what to do. “So if I win the bet, will I ever get this infamous kiss? I don’t want to miss out on it.”

Colin narrowed his gaze at her. “How about this? How about I give you a little taste of how amazing it will be right now? That should be enough to tide you over until I’ve won.”

She certainly couldn’t turn down an offer like that, especially knowing that his talented mouth and hands would distract her from everything else she was worried about. "All right," she agreed. "Lay one on me."

Colin shook his head at her. "Before I do that, I think we'd better adjourn to the bedroom."

"Why is that?" Natalie asked. "It's just a kiss."

"You say that, but this won't be an ordinary kiss. You'll be glad we waited until we're in there, I promise."

"Okay." She wasn't sure if he could deliver on the hype, but she was looking forward to finding out. Taking his hand, she led him up the stairs and down the hallway to her master bedroom.

Her bedroom had been what sold her on the townhouse. The master was spacious with large windows that let in the morning light. Even filled with her furniture, there was plenty of room to move around. "All right," she said, standing beside the bed with her hands on her hips. "Let's get a sampling of this infamous kiss of yours."

Colin moved closer and Natalie couldn't help but tense up. She didn't know what to expect. This wasn't even *the* kiss and she was nervous with anticipation.

"You look like I'm about to eat you alive," he said with an amused smile.

"Sorry," she said, trying to shake the tension out of her arms.

"That's okay." He stopped in front of her, just shy of touching. Instead of leaning in to kiss her, he turned her around and undid the zipper of her dress. He eased it off her shoulders, letting it pool to the floor.

"What are you doing?" she asked, curiously. What kind of kiss required her to be naked?

Leaning in, Colin growled in her ear, "I'm about to eat you alive."

Natalie gasped at the harsh intensity of his words, even as a thrill of need ran through her body. Before she could respond, he unclasped her bra and pulled her panties to the floor. Completely naked, she turned around to complain about the unfairness, but found he was busily ridding himself of his clothing as well. In a few moments, it was all tossed aside and he pulled her close.

"When is the kissing going to start?" she asked.

"You ask too many questions. This isn't a wedding you're in charge of. There are no schedules, tablets and earpieces tonight. Go with it."

"Yes, sir," Natalie said with a sheepish smile. Admittedly, she had trouble letting go and not knowing every aspect of the plan. She didn't think she had anything to worry about here, so she tried to turn off her brain and just let Colin take the lead. That was the whole point tonight, anyway.

His fingers delved into her hair as he leaned in for the kiss. Natalie braced herself for the earth-shattering impact, but at first at least, it was just a kiss. He coaxed her mouth open, letting his tongue slide along hers. His fingers massaged the nape of her neck as he tasted and nibbled at her.

Then she felt him start to pull away. His lips left hers, but technically, they never lost contact with her skin. He planted kisses along the line of her jaw, the hollow of her ear and down her throat. He crouched lower, nipping at her collarbone and placing a searing kiss between her breasts. He tasted each nipple, then continued down her soft belly until he was on his knees in front of her.

He placed a searing kiss at her hipbone, then the soft skin just above the cropped dark curls of her sex. Natalie gripped Colin's shoulders for support as his fingers slid between her thighs. She gasped softly as he stroked the wet heat that ached for him.

With his mouth still trailing across her thigh, Colin gently parted her with his fingers. His tongue immediately sought out her sensitive core, wrenching a desperate cry from Natalie's throat. He braced her hips with his hands as her knees threatened to give out beneath her.

She wasn't sure how much of this she could take. Standing up added a level of tension she hadn't expected. "Colin," she gasped, amazed by how her cries were growing more desperate with every second that passed.

She was on the edge, and it was clear that he intended to push her over it. Gripping her hip with one hand, he used the other to dip a finger inside her. The combination was explosive and Natalie couldn't hold back any longer. She threw her head back and cried out, her body thrashing against him with the power of her orgasm.

When it was over, Natalie slid to her knees in front of him. She lay her head on his shoulder, gasping and clinging to his biceps with both hands. She was so out of it, it took her a moment to realize Colin had picked her up. He helped her stand, then carried her to the bed only a few feet away.

"That," she panted as reason came back to her, "was one hell of a kiss."

"And that wasn't even the winning kiss," Colin said as he covered her body with his own.

"I can't even imagine it, then. It seems odd that your prize would be more a reward for me than for you."

He slipped inside her, making her overstimulated nerves spark with new sensation. "I assure you I enjoyed every second of it now, and I'll enjoy every second of it when I've won."

For that, Natalie had no response. She could only lift her hips to meet his forward advance. Clinging to him, she buried her face in his neck. His movements were slow, but forceful, a slow burn that would eventually consume everything it touched. She didn't resist the fire; she gave in to it.

She was tired of fighting. She had spent her whole life trying to protect herself from the pain and disappointment of love. She'd fought her urges for companionship, suppressed her jealousy as each of her friends found a great love she was certain she would never have.

And yet, here she was. Despite all the fighting and worrying, she had simply been overpowered. Gretchen was right. Natalie was in love.

"Oh Natalie," Colin groaned in her ear.

She loved that sound. She wanted to hear it again and again. Her name on his lips was better than a symphony orchestra.

Placing her hand against his cheek, she guided his mouth back to hers. That connection seemed to light a fire in him. Their lips still touching, he moved harder and faster than before, sweeping them both up in a massive wave of pleasure. Natalie didn't fight the currents, she just held on to the man in her arms, knowing she was safe there.

She never wanted to let go. But could she dare to hold on?

Ten

"I can't believe we're almost done with the house," Natalie said. "You've worked wonders on it."

Colin smiled. "I'm pretty pleased with the results."

"Seems a shame you can't keep it after all the work you've put in. You don't appear to care much for your own house. This place suits you more."

That was probably true, but he didn't need this place. "I can always buy another house. I'd like to see Lily and Frankie raise their family here."

"What is left for us to do?" Natalie asked as she looked around.

"I have to clean out my parents' office. I left that for last because there's so much paperwork to go through. I need to figure out what should be kept. I'm hoping we can shred most of it, but I really have no idea what they had stored away in all those drawers."

"Let's do it, then."

They walked up the stairs together and Colin opened the door to the small, dusty room he'd avoided the longest. Turning on the overhead light illuminated the big old oak desk on the far wall. It had two large file drawers, one on each side, housing any number of documents and files they'd thought were important to keep. It took up most of the space like a large man in a small dressing room.

Colin had lots of memories of his dad going over invoices at this desk long before Russell Landscaping could afford their own offices, much less their own office building in the city. This was where his mother wrote checks to pay the bills and managed correspondence. She hadn't been a big fan of email, always penning handwritten letters to friends and family.

There was also a large bookshelf on one wall with all his father's books. His dad had always been a big reader. He loved to curl up in his chair by the fireplace and read in the evenings. Volumes of books lined the shelves, and Colin dreaded going through them. As much as he felt the urge, he didn't need to keep them all, just a couple of his father's favorites.

"I'll take the shelves if you want to start on the drawers," Colin suggested. "We can throw out all the office supplies."

They each started their tasks. Natalie filled a wastebin with dried-up pens, markers and old, brittle rubber bands. After that, she started sorting through the file drawers.

Colin easily found his father's favorite book—*Treasure Island.* His father had read, and reread, that book twenty times. It was his favorite, as evidenced by the worn binding and fraying edges. He set that book aside.

It would go on Colin's shelf until he passed it on to his children. Other volumes weren't quite as important.

Colin quickly built up a stack of books to keep, then another to donate. He scooped up a handful for charity and turned, noticing Natalie sitting stone still in the office chair. The expression on her face was one of utter devastation.

"Natalie?" he asked. "What is it?"

Looking up at him, she bit at her lip. "It's…um." She stopped, shuffling through the papers. "I started going through the filing drawers. It looks like your mother actually filed for divorce."

Colin's breath caught in his lungs. He set the books down on the desk before he dropped them. "What? You must be reading it wrong."

Natalie handed over the folder. "I don't think so. It looks like your mother filed two years before their accident."

Colin flipped through the paperwork, coming to the same conclusion despite how much it pained him. His parents didn't divorce. What was this about? Leaning back onto the desk, he tried to make sense of it all.

"It looks like she started the process, but they didn't go through with it." Somehow that still didn't make him feel much better.

"I'm sorry to hear they were in a bad place," Natalie said. "I never noticed anything wrong as a kid, but in my experience, there's no perfect marriage. Everyone has problems, despite how they might look from the outside."

Colin set down the pages and frowned. "Of course there's no perfect marriage. Just because I want to marry and have a family someday doesn't mean I think it's going to be a walk in the park. You have to work at it every day because love is a choice. But it's a choice worth making. And judging by this paperwork, it's worth fighting to keep it."

"How do you get that? I always thought your parents had a good relationship. If even they filed for divorce at one point, I don't see that as a positive sign."

"What's positive is the fact that they *didn't* get a divorce. Things got ugly, but they decided not to give up. That makes me hopeful, not disappointed. If my mother could go as far as filing for divorce and they managed to put the pieces back together, that means there's hope for any marriage."

Judging by the look on Natalie's face, he could tell she wasn't convinced. She was so jaded by other people's relationship failures that she couldn't fathom two people actually loving each other enough to fight through the tough times.

That worried him. Despite what he'd overheard at Amelia's Christmas party, he didn't feel that confident that Natalie would stay in his life. She might love him, but she was still a flight risk. When this wedding was over, the two of them might be over, too. That was the thought that kept his feelings in check when they were together.

"You know what?" he said. "Let's just put all these files in a box and I'll go through them later. I think clearing the room out is time better spent."

Natalie just nodded and started unloading files from the desk drawer into the file boxes he'd bought. They worked silently together until the room was empty of personal items, and then they hauled the boxes downstairs and into his truck.

The mood for the night had been spoiled and he hated that. His parents' near-divorce was hanging over his head, opening his eyes to things he'd never considered. It seemed strange to drink some wine and go on like he didn't know the truth.

And yet, it made him feel emboldened, too. He'd gone into this whole situation with Natalie consciously holding back. It was defensive, to keep himself from getting in too deep and getting hurt, but it also occurred to him that it might be a self-fulfilling prophecy. If he didn't give all of himself to Natalie, she wouldn't ever do the same.

If he wanted to keep Natalie in his life, he had to fight for her and be bold. His parents fought to stay together, and he was willing to do the same. But what would give her the confidence to believe in him and their relationship? She was so determined to think of marriage as a mistake that most people struggled to get out of. How could he convince her that he was in this for the long haul and she shouldn't be afraid to love him with all she had?

There was only one thing he could think of, and it was a major risk. But, as his father told him once, no risk, no reward. That philosophy had helped him build the family landscaping business into a multimillion-dollar operation across the Southeast. He had no doubt it would succeed. If he could pull it off, there was no way Natalie could turn her nose up at it.

Just like his Christmas bet, he intended to get everything that he wanted and make it into something Natalie wanted, too. He knew exactly what he needed to do. The timing couldn't be more perfect.

"What are you doing Wednesday night?" he asked.

* * *

Natalie looked out the window at the twinkling Christmas lights up ahead and knew exactly where they were. "Are you taking me to the Opryland Hotel?" Natalie asked.

"Actually, no, we're going someplace else."

Sitting back in her seat, she watched as Colin slowed and pulled into the parking area for the Grand Ole Opry. At that moment, she perked up, her mind spinning as she tried to figure out what day it was. It was the sixteenth. Blake Wright's concert was here tonight. But it was sold out…

"Colin?" she asked.

"Yes?"

"Did you…? Are we…?" She was so excited she couldn't even form the words. Why else would they be here if he hadn't managed to get tickets to the show?

"Yes, I did and yes, we are," he answered, pulling into a parking space.

She almost couldn't believe it. "There were no tickets left. They sold out in ten minutes. I know—I called."

Colin nodded as he turned off the car and faced her. "You're absolutely right. There were no seats left."

Natalie narrowed her gaze at him. "So, what? We're just going to lurk by the back door to see if we can get a glimpse of him?" She was willing to do that, of course, but it didn't seem like Colin's style.

"Something like that. Come on."

They got out of the car and he took her hand, leading her away from the crowd at the entrance and around the building toward the back. The door they were headed for said Private Entry in big red letters, and a very large man in a tight T-shirt stood watch. Colin didn't seem to care. He marched right up to him and pulled two tickets out of his jacket.

No, wait. Natalie looked closer. They weren't tickets. They were *backstage passes*. The security guard looked them over and checked the list on his clipboard.

"Welcome, Mr. Russell. So glad to have you joining us tonight." The mountain of a man stepped aside and let Natalie and Colin go into the sacred backstage of the famous concert hall.

She waited until the door shut before she lost her cool. "Are you kidding me? Backstage? We're going backstage at a Blake Wright concert? This is the Grand Ole Opry! Do you know how many amazing artists have walked where we are right now?"

Colin wasn't left with much time to answer her questions, so he just smiled and let her freak out. Passes in hand, they walked through the preconcert chaos until they located the stage manager.

"Looks like our special guests are here," the man said. "Welcome, folks. We've got two designated seats for you right over here." He indicated two chairs just off the curtained stage area. They were going to be watching the show from the wings, literally sitting unseen on the stage itself.

Natalie was so excited, she could barely sit down. Colin had to hold her hand to keep her from popping right up out of her seat. "Please tell me how you managed this," she said at last.

"Well, you know who does all the landscaping for Gaylord properties?"

She had no idea. "You?" she guessed.

"That is correct. Russell Landscaping has the contract to design and maintain all the outdoor spaces including the hotel and the concert venue. I called up a friend here and they set this up for me. Since there weren't any seats left, we had to get a little creative."

Natalie could hardly believe it. "This is amazing. I can't believe you did all this. I mean, you already gave me my Christmas present. What is this for?"

Colin shrugged. "Because I could. You told me how your dad used to take you and how much you liked Blake, so I thought it would be a nice gesture."

"Well, I'm glad I dressed appropriately," she said, looking over her off-the-shoulder red silk top and skinny jeans with cowboy boots. "You just said we were going someplace to listen to country music. I was thinking maybe a bar downtown."

"Well, I would've given away the surprise if I'd said anything else."

Natalie could only shake her head. As the opening act brushed past them to go out onstage, she muffled her squeal of delight in Colin's coat sleeve.

When Blake and his band finally took the stage, it took everything she had not to jump up and down. She tried to play it cool, since she was here because of Colin's business connections, but it was very hard. Natalie could hold her composure during any kind of wedding crisis, but this was too much.

It was not just a great concert, but there were so many memories centered around this place. Her parents had been house poor, putting everything they had into a nice home for their family at the expense of everything else. They didn't have the latest gadgets or the coolest clothes, but she went to a good school and had everything she truly needed.

But once a year, around her birthday, her dad always

took her out for what he called a Daddy-Daughter date. She'd grown up listening to his favorite country music, and starting on her fifth birthday, he took her to a show at the Opry. It didn't matter who it was or that they had the worst seats in the house. It was more about sharing something with her father.

That tradition had fallen to the wayside after the divorce, and it had broken Natalie's heart. She hadn't stepped foot back into this concert hall since the last time her daddy brought her here.

And now, here she was, backstage. She didn't talk to her father very often, but she couldn't wait to tell him about this. He'd be amazed. Maybe it would even inspire him to take another trip here with her for old times' sake.

Glancing over at Colin, she realized he looked a little anxious and not at all like he was having a good time. He was stiff, clutching his knees and not so much as tapping his toes to the music. "You don't like country music, do you?" she asked.

"Oh no," he argued. "It's fine. I'm just tired."

Natalie didn't worry too much about it, focusing on the amazing show. About halfway through, Blake started introducing the next song.

"The song I'm going to play next was one of my biggest hits," he said. "It was my first real love song, written about my wife. I want to dedicate this song tonight to a very special lady. Natalie Sharpe, please come out onto the stage."

Natalie's heart stopped in her chest. Colin tried to pull her up out of her seat, but it took a moment for her to connect everything. "Me?" she asked, but he gave her a little shove and suddenly, she was onstage where everyone could see her.

"There she is," Blake said. "Come on out here, sugar."

Natalie walked stiffly over to where Blake was standing. Under her feet were the very boards of the original stage. The lights were shining on her, the crowd cheering. She thought she might pass out.

"Are you enjoying the show?" he asked.

"Absolutely. You're awesome," she said.

Blake laughed. "Well, thank you. Do you know who else is awesome? Colin Russell. Colin, why don't you come on out here, too?"

Natalie turned and watched Colin walk out onstage. What the heck was going on? Her life had suddenly become very surreal. It was one thing for Colin to arrange for her to get to go out onstage with her idol. Both of them onstage changed everything.

Blake slapped Colin on the back. "Now, Colin tells me he has something he wants to ask you."

The whole crowed started cheering louder. The blood rushed into Natalie's ears, drowning out everything but her heart's rapid thump. She barely had time to react, her body moving like it was caught in molasses. She looked over at Colin just in time to see him slip down onto one knee. *Oh dear, sweet Jesus.* He wasn't. He couldn't be. This was not happening.

"Natalie," Colin began, "I've known you since we were teenagers. When you came back into my life, I knew you were someone special. The more time we spend together, the more I realize that I want to spend all my time with you, for the rest of my life. I love you, Natalie Sharpe. Will you marry me?"

Now Natalie was certain she was going to pass out.

She could feel the whole concert hall start to spin. Her chest grew tight, her cheeks burned. What was he thinking? All these people were watching. Blake was watching…

Colin held up the ring. It was beautiful—a large oval diamond set in platinum with a pear-shaped diamond flanking it on each side. The cut and clarity were amazing. The stone glittered with the lights on the stage, beckoning her to reach out and take it. All she had to do was say yes, and he would slip it on her finger.

And then what? They'd get married and last a few years at best? Then they'd get divorced and spend months squabbling in court? In the end, she'd become a bitter divorcée and sell this same beautiful ring in a ranting ad on Craigslist.

Yes, she loved him, but why did they have to get married? He was ruining everything they'd built together by changing their whole relationship dynamic. Love or no, she couldn't do it. She just couldn't get the words out. All she knew was that she had to get out of here. Avoiding his gaze, Natalie shook her head. "No. I'm sorry, I can't," she said, before turning and running off the stage.

As she ran, she was only aware of an eerie silence. The entire concert hall had quieted. The crew backstage all stood around in stunned confusion. Apparently no one had expected her to reject his proposal.

"Natalie!" she heard Colin yell, but she couldn't stop. She weaved in and out of people and equipment, desperately searching for the side door where they'd come in. Just as she found it, she heard the music start playing again. Life went on for everyone else, just as her life started to unravel.

Bursting through the doors, she took in a huge gulp of cool air that she desperately needed. The security guard watched her curiously as she bent over and planted her hands on her knees for support.

Marriage? He'd proposed marriage! He'd taken a perfectly wonderful evening and ruined it with those silly romantic notions. Why did he do that?

"Natalie?" Colin said as he came out the door behind her a moment later.

She turned around to face him, not sure what to say. She felt the prickle of tears start to sting her eyes. "What were you thinking?" she asked. "You know how I feel about marriage!"

"I was thinking that you loved me and wanted to be with me," he replied, his own face reddening with emotion.

"We had an agreement, Colin. We were not going to fall in love. This was supposed to be fun and easy."

"That's how it started, but it changed. For both of us. Tell me you love me, Natalie. Don't lie about it, not now."

She took a deep breath, trying to get the words out of her mouth for the first time. "I do love you," she said. "But that doesn't change my answer. I don't want to get married. That just ruins everything that we have going so perfectly right now. I've told you before I don't believe in marriage. Proposing out of the blue makes me think you don't listen to me at all. If you did, you never would've done something like…like…"

"Something so romantic and thoughtful?" he suggested. "Something so perfect and special to commemorate the moment so you'd never forget it? Something that a woman that truly loved me could never turn down?"

"Something so public!" she shouted instead. "Did you think that you could twist my arm into accepting your proposal by having four thousand witnesses? You proposed to me onstage in front of Blake Wright! All those people watching us." She shook her head, still in disbelief that the night had taken such a drastic turn. "That whole thing is probably going to end up on the internet and go viral."

Colin's hands curled into controlled fists at his sides. She could see the ring box still in one hand. "Is that what you think I was doing with all of this? I couldn't possibly have been trying to craft the perfect moment to start our lives together. Obviously, I was just *coercing you* into marrying me, because that worked out so well for me the first time."

It was perfect. It had been perfect. And if she was any other woman, it would've been the kind of story she would've told her grandchildren about. But she couldn't pull the trigger. This was too much, too soon. She'd just come to terms with loving him; she wasn't ready to sign her life away to this man. They might have known each other since they were kids, but how much did they really know about each other?

"You hardly know me, and yet you want to change me. If you really loved me, Colin, you wouldn't force me into something I don't want to do. You would understand that I need time for a step this big, and that I might never want to make that leap."

He ran his hand through his hair in incredulity. "Yes, I'm such a horrible person for inviting you to be a part of my family and to let me love you forever. What a bastard I am!"

Natalie stopped, his beautiful, yet rage-filled words

sending a tear spilling down her cheek. There was no stopping the tears now, and she hated that. She hated to cry more than anything else. How had this perfect night gone so wrong? "You can do all that without a marriage."

"But why would I want to? It doesn't make any sense, Natalie. Why can't you make that commitment to me? You know, I always thought you were such a strong woman. So in control, so self-assured. But in reality, you're a damn coward."

"What?" she asked through her tears.

"You heard me. You hide behind this big philosophical cover story about love and marriage being this forced social paradigm and whatever other crap you've recited because you're afraid of getting hurt. You're afraid to give in and let someone love you, then have it not work out."

Natalie didn't know what to say to that. It was true. She'd justified her own fears in her mind with all the statistics and academic findings she could spew. But the truth was that she used it all to keep men away. She'd done a hell of a job this time. She didn't want to lose Colin entirely, though. Couldn't they just go back to before he proposed? Pretend like tonight never happened?

"I might be scared to take the leap, but what if I'm right? What if I'd said yes and we had this big wedding and four kids and one day, we wake up and hate each other?"

"And what if we don't? What if we do all of that and we're actually happy together for the rest of our lives? Did you ever consider that option while you were wringing your hands?"

Did she dare consider it? Her mom considered it over

and over just to fail. Time had turned her into a bitter woman constantly searching for something to complete her. Natalie wouldn't let herself become like that. "I'm sorry, Colin. I just can't take that chance."

Colin stuffed his hands in his pockets, his posture stiff and unyielding. "Don't be sorry. If you don't want to marry me, that's fine. It doesn't matter what your reasoning is. But I'm done with the two of us. One marriage to a reluctant bride is enough for me. Come on, I'll drive you home."

"I think I should take a cab. That would be easier on us both."

She saw the shimmer of tears in his eyes for just a moment before he turned and walked away. Natalie could only stand and watch as he got into his car and drove away.

As his taillights disappeared into the distance, Natalie felt her heart start to crumble in her chest. She'd been so afraid to love and be loved that she had driven Colin away and made her fears a reality.

With one simple *no*, Natalie had ruined everything.

Eleven

Colin avoided going to the chapel for as long as he could. He didn't want to see Natalie. He didn't want to spend most of the evening with her, pretending everything was fine for the benefit of his sister and her fiancé. Like any injured animal, he wanted to stay in his den and lick his wounds alone.

The worst part was that he knew he'd done this to himself. Natalie had been very clear on the fact that she never wanted to get married and yet, he'd proposed to her anyway. He'd thought perhaps it was some sort of defense mechanism, insisting she didn't want it so people wouldn't pity her for not having it.

Overhearing her confession to Gretchen of being in love with him had given him a false hope. Somehow, he'd believed that offering her his heart and a lifetime commitment would not only show her he was serious, but that she had nothing to fear. That hadn't panned out at all.

What was wrong with him? Why was he so attracted to women who didn't want the same things he wanted? It was like he was subconsciously setting himself up for failure. Maybe *he* was the one who was really afraid of being hurt, so he chose women he could never really have. What a mess.

Pulling his truck into the parking lot of the chapel, he parked but didn't get out. The rehearsal was supposed to start in twenty minutes. No need to rush in just because there was no sense in going all the way home first.

Glancing out the window, he looked around at the other cars. He spotted Natalie's sports car, plus a handful of other vehicles he didn't recognize. There were no motorcycles, though. And no little hatchback. Where were Lily and Frankie?

Reaching for his phone, he dialed his sister's number. "Hello?" she shouted over a dull roar of noise around her.

"Lily, where are you?"

"We're stuck in the Vegas airport. Our flight got cancelled because of bad weather in Denver. We've been changed to a new flight, but it's not leaving until tomorrow morning."

"Tomorrow morning? You're going to miss the rehearsal and the dinner." Colin knew the weather wasn't Lily's fault, but things like this always seemed to happen when she was involved. Who booked a flight that connected through Denver in the winter, anyway?

"I know, Colin!" she snapped. "We're not going to make it in time for your choreographed circus. That's why I called Natalie first and told her. She said she'd handle things tonight and go over the details with us tomorrow afternoon before the service. We're doing what we can. It isn't the end of the world."

Nothing was ever a big deal to Lily. She said Colin was wrapped too tight and needed to loosen up, but he would counter that she needed to take some things—like her wedding day—more seriously.

"Just cancel the rehearsal dinner reservations," she continued. "It was only the wedding party and Frankie's parents, anyway."

That he could do. Thank goodness they hadn't opted for the big catered dinner with out-of-town guests. "Fine. You promise you'll be back tomorrow?"

"I can't control the weather, Colin. We'll get back as soon as we can."

Colin hung up the phone, a feeling of dread pooling in his gut. He was beginning to think this entire thing was a mistake. Lily didn't want this wedding, and he'd twisted her arm. If he hadn't done that, he wouldn't have made such a calculated error with Natalie. Lily would be happily courthouse married. He wouldn't have learned the truth about his parents' marriage yet. There also wouldn't be an extremely expensive diamond engagement ring in his coat pocket.

He needed to take it back to the jeweler, but he hadn't had the heart to do it. He'd return it on Monday when all of this was over. That would close the book on this whole misguided adventure and then, maybe, he could move on.

With a sigh, he opened the door and slipped out of the truck. After talking to Lily, he knew he needed to get inside and see what needed to be done to compensate for the absence of the engaged couple.

Inside the chapel, things were hopping. The doors to the reception hall were propped open for vendors to come in and out with decorations. He could see Gretchen and the photographer, Bree, putting out place settings on the tables. A produce truck was unloading crates of fruits and vegetables into the kitchen.

Natalie was in the center of the chaos, as always. She was setting out name cards shaped like snowflakes on a table in the crossroads of the chapel entrance. A large white tree was on the table in front of her, dripping with crystals, pearls and twinkle lights. She was stringing silver ribbon through each name card and then hanging it from a branch on the tree, creating a sparkling blizzard effect.

She reached for another, hesitating as she noticed Colin standing a few feet away. "Have you spoken with your sister?" she asked, very cold and professional once again.

"Yes. Will we still have a rehearsal?"

"Yes." Natalie set down a snowflake and turned toward him. "It's not just for the benefit of the bride and groom. It helps the pastor, the musicians and the rest of the wedding party. They only have a best man and maid of honor, so it might be a short rehearsal, but it's still needed to get everyone else comfortable with the flow."

"Are the others here?"

"We're just waiting on the maid of honor."

"What about the parts for the bride and groom in the ceremony?"

"We'll have to get someone to stand in for them both. I've had to do this before—it's not a big deal. I had a bride get food poisoning, and she missed everything leading up to the ceremony. It all turned out fine."

"Okay." Her confidence made him feel better despite the anxious tension in his shoulders. "I'll stand in for Frankie, if you need me to. I'm not in the wedding party, so I don't have anything else to do."

Natalie smiled politely and reached for her paper snowflake again. "Thanks for volunteering. You can go into the chapel and wait with the others if you like. We'll begin momentarily."

Even though he was angry with her, he couldn't stand to see the blank, detached expression on her face when she looked at him. He wanted to see those dark brown eyes filled with love, or even just the light of passion or laughter. He wanted to reach out and shake her until she showed any kind of emotion. Anger, fear, he didn't care. She had been so afraid to feel anything before they met. He worried that after their blowup, she'd completely retreat into herself. He might not be the one who got to love her for the rest of her life, but someone should.

Natalie would have to let someone, however, and he had no control over that.

He wanted to say something to her. Anything. But he didn't want to start another fight here. Instead, he nodded and disappeared into the chapel to wait with the others. That was the best thing to do if they were going to get through all this without more turmoil than they already had.

The maid of honor walked in a few minutes later with Natalie on her heels. She had her headset on and her stiff, purposeful walk had returned.

"Okay, everyone, I'm going to go over this once, quickly, then we will walk through the whole ceremony so everyone gets a feel for their roles and how it will all go."

Colin stood with his arms crossed over his chest as she handed out instructions to the string quartet in the corner, the ushers and the wedding party.

"Colin is our stand-in groom today. After you escort in your parents, you and the best man are going to follow the pastor in and wait at the front of the church for the ceremony to start. Everyone ready?"

All the people in the chapel, excepting the musicians, went out into the hall. Colin and the best man, Steve, followed Pastor Greene into the chapel, taking their places on the front platform. The string quartet played a soothing melody that sounded familiar, but he didn't know the name. At the back of the room, Natalie gave a cue to the pastor before slipping into the vestibule. He asked everyone to rise. The musicians transitioned to a different song, playing louder to announce the coming of the bridal party.

The doors opened and the maid of honor made her way down the aisle. She moved to the opposite side of the landing and waited for the doors to open a final time. The music built a sense of anticipation that made Colin anxious to see what was about to happen, even as a stand-in groom for a rehearsal.

The doors of the chapel swung open, and standing there holding a bouquet of silk flowers, was Natalie. His chest tightened as she walked down the aisle toward him. She was wearing a burgundy silk blouse and a black pencil skirt instead of a white gown, but it didn't matter. The moment was all too real to Colin.

But with every step she took, reality sunk in even more. This wasn't their rehearsal and they weren't getting married. She had turned him down, flat, in front of a couple thousand people and a country music star.

The sentimental feelings quickly dissipated, the muscles in his neck and shoulders tightening with irritation and anger.

Natalie avoided his gaze as she approached the platform. She looked only at the pastor. Her full lips were thin and pressed hard into a line of displeasure. Neither of them seemed very happy to have to go through all this so soon after their blowup.

This was going to be an interesting rehearsal.

Natalie wished there was someone else to fill in for Lily, but there just wasn't. Everyone else was preparing for tomorrow and Bree was capturing everything—including her awkward moments with Colin—on camera. All she could do was man up, grab the dummy bouquet and march down the aisle so they could get through this.

"Frankie will take Lily's hand and help her up onto the platform," the pastor explained. "Lily will pass her bouquet to the maid of honor to hold, then I will read the welcome passages about marriage."

Natalie took Colin's hand, ignoring the thrill that ran up her arm as they touched. She clenched her teeth as she handed off the bouquet and listened to the pastor go through his spiel. They had opted for the traditional, nondenominational Christian service, passing on any long biblical passages. Colin had insisted that Lily didn't want to stand up here for a drawn-out religious service. She wanted to get married and then cue the party.

"When I finish, Frankie and Lily will turn to face each other and hold hands while they recite the vows."

This was the part Natalie was dreading. Turning to Colin, she took the other hand he offered. It was awkward to stare at his chest, so she forced her chin up to meet his eyes. The initial contact was like a punch to her stomach. There wasn't a hint of warmth in those golden eyes. He hated her, and she understood that. She had thrown his love in his face. She didn't know what else to do. Say yes? Dive headfirst into the fantasy of marriage like everyone else? She could see now how easy it was to get swept up into it. The current was strong.

Even now, as they stood on the altar together, she felt her body start to relax and her resistance fade. Colin repeated Frankie's vows, the words of love and trust making Natalie's chest ache. His expression softened as he spoke, slipping a pretend ring onto her finger.

When it was her turn to recite Lily's vows, the anxiety was gone. She felt a sense of peace standing here with Colin, as though that was where they were truly meant to be. She loved him. She was scared, but she loved him and had loved him since she was fifteen years old. She'd never felt this way for anyone else because of that. Her heart was already taken, so why would she have any desire to love or marry another man?

She wanted to marry Colin. There was no question of it now. Why did she have to have this revelation two days too late?

She felt her hands start to tremble in his as her voice began to shake as well. Colin narrowed his gaze at her, squeezing her hands tighter to calm the tremble. She was glad to have an imaginary ring, because she was certain she would've dropped any real jewelry trying to put it on his finger.

Natalie felt tears form in her eyes as the pastor talked about their holy vows. She wanted to interrupt the rehearsal, to blurt out right then and there that she was wrong. She was sorry for letting her fears get in the way. And most important, that she very desperately wanted to marry him.

"I'll pronounce them man and wife, then instruct Frankie to kiss the bride," the pastor explained. "They'll kiss, holding together long enough for the photographer to get a good shot. Then Lily will get her bouquet and the couple will turn out to face the congregation. I'll announce them as Mr. and Mrs. Frank Watson, and then you'll exit the chapel."

The musicians started playing the exit song. Colin offered his arm and she took it. They stepped down the stairs and along the aisle to the back of the chapel.

When they walked through the doorway, he immediately pulled away from her. She instantly missed the warmth and nearness of his touch, but she knew the moment had passed. The Colin standing beside her now hated her once again.

She recovered by returning to her professional duties. Shc waited until the maid of honor and best man came out of the chapel behind them, then she returned to the doorway, clapping. "Great job everyone. Now, at this point, the bridal party will be escorted away so the guests can move into the reception hall, then we'll bring you back into the chapel to take pictures. Does anyone have any questions?"

Everyone shook their heads. It was a small wedding and not particularly complicated aside from the absence of the bride and groom. "Great. Let's make sure everyone is here at the chapel by three tomorrow. We'll do some pictures with Bree before the ceremony. If anything happens, you all have my cell phone number."

People started scattering from the room, Colin

amongst them. “Colin?” she called out to him before she lost her nerve.

He stopped and turned back to face her. “Yes?”

“Can I talk to you for a minute?”

“About what?” She’d never seen him so stiff and unfriendly. It was even worse than it had been before the rehearsal. “Everything for the wedding is set, isn’t it?”

“Yes, of course.”

“Then we have nothing to talk about.”

His abrupt shutdown rattled her. “I, I mean, could you please just give me two minutes to talk about what happened at the concert?”

He shook his head, his jaw so tight it was like stone. “I think you said all you needed to say on that stage, don’t you?”

She had said a lot, but she had said all the wrong things. “No. Please, Colin. You don’t understand how much I—”

He held up his hand to silence her. “Natalie, stop. You don’t want to marry me. That’s fine. I’m through with trying to convince unwilling women to be my wife. But like I said that night, I’m done. I don’t want to discuss it ever again. Let’s just forget it ever happened so we can get through this wedding without any more drama, okay?”

Before she could answer, Colin turned and disappeared from the chapel. Natalie heard the chime as he opened the front door and headed for his truck.

With every step he took, she felt her heart sink further into her stomach. Her knees threatened to give out from under her, forcing her to sit down in one of the rear pews. She held it together long enough for the musicians to leave, but once she was alone, she completely came undone.

It had been a long time since Natalie cried—good and cried. She got teary at the occasional commercial or news article. She'd shed a tear with Amelia when she lost her first baby in the spring and a few at the concert the other night. But nothing like this. Not since… she paused in her tears to think. Not since her father left Christmas day.

She dropped her face into her hands, trying not to ugly sob so loudly that it echoed through the chapel. There were a lot of people going in and out of the building today, but she didn't want anyone to see her in such a wretched state.

"Natalie?" a voice called from behind her, as if on cue.

She straightened to attention, wiping her eyes and cheeks without smearing her mascara. "Yes?" she replied without turning around to expose her red, puffy face. "What do you need?"

Natalie sensed the presence move closer until she noticed Gretchen standing at the entrance of the pew beside her. "I need you to scoot over and tell me what the hell is going on."

She complied, knowing there was no way out of this now. Gretchen settled into the seat, politely keeping her gaze trained on the front of the chapel. She didn't say a word, waiting for Natalie to spill her guts on her own time.

"I like Christmas," Natalie confessed. "I like the lights and the food and the music. My holiday humbug days are behind me."

"What? That's why you're crying?"

"Yes. No. Yes and no. I'm crying because I've finally found my Christmas spirit and it doesn't matter. None of it matters because Colin and I are over."

Gretchen groaned in disappointment. "What happened? You seemed pretty enamored with him a few days ago."

"He…proposed. Onstage at the Blake Wright concert. In front of everyone."

"Well, I could see how a lifetime promise of love and devotion in front of thousands of witnesses could ruin a relationship."

Natalie noted her friend's flat tone. "I panicked. And I said no. And I didn't do it well. I said some pretty ugly things to him."

Gretchen put her arm around Natalie's shoulder. "Why are you fighting this so hard? What are you afraid of, Natalie?"

"I'm afraid…" She took a deep breath. "I'm afraid that I'm going to let myself fall for the fantasy and he's going to leave."

"The fantasy?" Gretchen questioned.

"Love. Marriage."

"How can you still see it as a fantasy when you know you're in love with him?"

"Because I can't be certain it's real. This could just be a biological attachment to ensure the care of my nonexistent offspring. And even if it is real, I can't be sure it will last."

"You can't be certain of anything in life, Natalie. Maybe it's biology, maybe it's not. But by pushing Colin away, you're guaranteeing that you're going to lose him. It doesn't matter if your feelings will last now."

"I know," Natalie said with a sigh. "I realized that

today when we were standing on the altar during the rehearsal. Up there, holding his hands and looking into his eyes, I realized that I want to be with Colin. I want to marry him. He's worth the risk. But it's too late. I've ruined everything. He won't even speak to me about anything but Lily's wedding."

"I think he might just need a little time. You've both got a lot on your minds with the wedding. They're so stressful. But once that's done, I say reach out to him. Put your heart on the line the way he did. Take the risk. If he says no, you haven't lost anything. But if you can get him to listen to how you feel, you can gain everything."

Natalie nodded and dried the last of her tears. Gretchen was right. How had she become a relationship expert so quickly?

She knew what she had to do now. She had to hand her heart to Colin on a silver platter and pray he didn't crush it.

Twelve

Colin was trying to keep his mind occupied. Just a few more hours and all this would be over. He could give the keys to the house to his sister, pay the bill for the wedding and walk out of this place like he'd never fallen in love with Natalie Sharpe.

Sure, it would be that easy.

He was busying himself by greeting guests as they came into the chapel. He assisted the ushers in handing out programs, hugging and kissing friends and family as they came in. A lot of folks had shown up for Lily's big day and he was pleased. They had sent out a lot of email invitations, but in the rush, he wasn't sure who had accepted until they walked in the door.

He was very surprised to see Natalie's mother and father walk into the chapel. They had big smiles on their faces as they chatted and made their way over to him.

Perhaps time and distance had healed their wounds, even if Natalie's remained fresh.

"Mr. Sharpe," Colin said, shaking the man's hand.

"How are you, son?"

"Doing well," he lied. "So glad you could make it for Lily and Frankie's big day."

He hugged Natalie's mother and the usher escorted them all down the aisle to their seats. Casually, he glanced at his watch. It was getting close to time. He'd expected to see Frankie by now, but every bearded, tattooed guy that caught his eye was just a guest of the groom.

Glancing across the foyer, he spotted Natalie and instantly knew that something was wrong. She looked decidedly flustered and he didn't expect that of her, even after everything that happened last night. She looked very put-together, as usual, in a light gray linen suit with her headset on and her crystal-encrusted tablet clutched to her chest, but there was an anxiety lining her dark eyes.

As much as he didn't want to talk to her, he made his way through the crowd of arriving wedding guests to where she was standing. "What's the matter?"

Taking him by the elbow, she led him into the hallway near her office where they were out of the guests' earshot. "They're not here yet."

"They who?"

"Your sister and her fiancé. The flight they were supposed to be on landed four hours ago, I checked, but I haven't heard a word from either of them. I've got a hair and makeup crew twiddling their thumbs. The wedding starts in thirty minutes and I've got no couple to marry."

An icy-cold fear started rushing through his veins. He'd worried about this almost from the moment he'd insisted that Lily have a formal wedding. It didn't surprise him at all. She'd given in to his request far too easily. He should've known she'd do something like this when the opportunity arose. "I'm sure they're on their way," he said, trying to soothe her nerves even as his lit up with panic. "This has to happen all the time, right?"

"No. It's *never* happened. I have had grooms bail, brides bail, but never both of them together. You've got to track her down. Now. She's not answering my calls."

"Okay. I'll try calling her right now." He stepped away from her office and went down the hall to the far corner where the sounds of the crowd wouldn't interfere. As he was about to raise the phone to his ear, it vibrated and chimed in his hand. When he looked down, it was like someone had kicked him in the stomach. The air was completely knocked out of him.

It was a photo text from his sister. She and Frankie were standing under the Chapel of Love sign, sporting wedding rings. They were wearing jeans. She had a little veil on her head and a carnation bouquet in her hand. "Guess what? We decided to stay in Vegas and elope! Sorry about the plans."

Sorry about the plans. His chest started to tighten. Sorry about the plans? There were two hundred people in the chapel, a staff in the kitchen preparing the dinner. There were *ten thousand dollars'* worth of flowers decorating the ballroom. That was just the ballroom! But the bride and groom decided to elope in Vegas. So sorry.

When he was finally able to look up from his phone, he caught Natalie's eye from across the hall. She looked the way he felt, with a distraught expression on her face. She held up her own phone to display the same picture he was looking at.

They moved quickly toward each other, meeting in the middle. "What do we do?"

Natalie took a deep breath. "Well, obviously there isn't going to be a wedding, so we can send the preacher home. The food and band are already paid for, and there's no sense in it all going to waste. So if I were you, I'd lie and tell them that Lily and Frankie got stuck in Vegas because of bad weather and decided to elope. Invite them to celebrate at the reception, have dinner, eat the cake and send everyone home."

Colin dropped his face into his hands. How had this week turned into such a disaster? His proposal to Natalie couldn't have gone worse. His sister was a no-show for her own wedding. He was feeling like he wanted to just walk out the door and lock himself in his bedroom until the New Year.

He supposed her suggestion was sensible. There was no point in wasting all that food. "I guess that's what we'll have to do, then. What a mess. I'm going to kill her when she gets home. I mean it."

"There is one other option," she said in a voice so small he almost didn't hear it.

Colin looked up to see Natalie nervously chewing at her lip. "What other option?"

She looked at him for a moment, a determined tilt to her chin that hadn't been there before. "This is going to sound crazy, but hear me out, okay?"

"At this point, I'm open to anything."

"I'm sorry, Colin. I'm sorry about the way I reacted to your proposal. I know I hurt you and I didn't intend to. But you were right, I was just scared. My whole life I've seen relationships fall apart and I told myself I'd never put myself through that. And then I fell in love with you anyway. I didn't know what to do. When you proposed, the moment was so perfect and I just panicked. I ruined it all and I can never tell you just how sorry I am. I would go back in time and change it if I could, but I can't."

Colin had certainly not been expecting this right now. With everything else going on, he wasn't entirely sure he was emotionally capable of handling her apology. "Natalie, can we talk about this later? I understand you want to get this off your chest, but we're in the middle of a crisis here."

"And I'm trying to fix it," she countered. "Do you love me, Colin?"

He looked down at her heart-shaped face, her brow furrowed in worry. The headset lined her cheek, the microphone hovering right at the corner of her full, pink lips. Of course he loved her. That was what hurt the most. They loved each other, but for some reason, everything had gone wrong and he didn't understand why. Although he didn't want to admit it, he figured it couldn't hurt at this point.

"Yes, I love you, Natalie. That's why I proposed to you. I wanted to start a life with you and I thought you wanted the same thing."

"I didn't know what I wanted, but now I do. I do want to start a life with you."

Colin barely had a chance to process Natalie's words before she dropped down onto one knee in front of him. "Natalie, what are you doing?"

"I love you, Colin. There's nothing I want more than to marry you and build a life together. I'm sorry that I ruined your grand proposal, but I have another one for you. Will you marry me?"

Colin looked around, trying to see if anyone was watching the bizarre scene in front of him. "Are you proposing to me?"

Natalie took his hand and held it tightly in her own. "Yes. I want to marry you, Colin. Right now."

He stiffened, then dropped down on his own knee, so they could discuss this eye to eye. "You want to get married right now?"

She smiled wide. "Why not? We've got a chapel full of your family just a few feet away. My parents are even here. The wedding gown fits me. Not to mention that we've got a big, beautiful reception waiting that you and I planned together. It's exactly the wedding I would choose if we were going to get married any other day. It's going to go to waste if we don't use it, so why not today?"

Colin's heart started racing in his chest. Would they really go through with this? "Natalie, are you sure? I can't bear to have another wife change her mind and walk out of my life. If we get married today, we're getting married forever. Are you okay with that?"

She reached out and cupped his face, holding his cheeks in her hands. "I am very okay with that. You're not getting rid of me, mister."

"Okay, then yes, I will marry you," he said with a grin. He leaned forward to kiss her, the mouthpiece of her headset getting in the way.

"Oops," Natalie said, lifting it up. "Just as well," she noted as she leaned back. "I think we need to save our next kiss for the one at the altar, don't you?"

It was entirely possible that Natalie had lost her mind. She wasn't just getting married, she was getting married on a whim. It was crazy. It was so unlike her.

And she'd never been more excited in her life.

She wanted this more than anything, and getting married quickly was the only thing that would keep her from sabotaging herself.

Natalie rushed toward the bridal suite, reaching out to grab Gretchen's arm and drag her down the hallway with her.

"Where are we going?" she asked. "I'm supposed to be fetching something for Bree."

She kept going. "Don't worry about Bree. I need you to help me get ready."

"Help you get ready to do what?"

"To marry Colin."

A sudden resistant weight stopped her forward progress and jerked her back. "Would you like to repeat that, please?"

Natalie sighed and turned toward her. "The bride and groom aren't coming. Colin and I are getting married instead. I need you to help me get dressed."

Gretchen's jaw dropped, but she followed her willingly to the bridal suite in a state of shock. The hair and makeup crew were loitering there, waiting for the missing bride.

"Change of plans, ladies," Natalie announced, pulling off her headset and tugging the band from her ponytail. "I'm the bride now. I need the best, fastest work you can do."

She settled down in the chair and the team quickly went to work. A soft knock came a few minutes later and Bree slipped in with her camera. "Are we ready to take some pictures of the bride getting read—?" Bree stopped short when she saw Natalie in the chair. "What's going on?"

"Natalie is getting married." Gretchen held up the cell phone picture of their wayward couple. "You're taking pictures of her and Colin instead."

Bree took a deep breath and started nervously adjusting the lens on her camera. "Well, okay then. You might want to give Amelia a heads-up in the meantime. She'll have a fit if she's in the kitchen and misses the ceremony."

Gretchen nodded and slipped out. Within about twenty minutes, Natalie was completely transformed. Her ponytail was brushed out, straightened and wrapped into a French twist. She was painted with classic cat eyes, dark lashes and rosy cheeks. They opted for a nude lip with a touch of sparkle.

By the time Gretchen returned, Natalie was ready to slip into the dress. "Colin has spoken to the pastor, so he's on board. I brought your dad out of the chapel to walk you down the aisle. He's waiting outside."

Perfect. That was an important detail she hadn't considered in her rash proposal. Thank goodness her parents were both here. She'd never hear the end of it if either of them had missed her wedding.

"Let's get you in this gown," Gretchen said.

It took a few minutes to get Natalie laced and buttoned into her wedding dress. The hairdresser positioned the veil in her hair and turned her toward the full-length mirror to look at herself.

Her heart stuttered in her chest when she saw her reflection. She made for a beautiful bride. And this time, unlike at the bridal salon, she was really going to be the bride. This was suddenly her day, and her gown. She was so happy they'd chosen this dress. Any other one just wouldn't have suited her.

"Wow, honey," Gretchen said. "You look amazing. Do you have heels?"

Natalie looked down at her sensible black flats and shook her head. That was one thing she didn't have. "I guess I'll just go barefoot," she replied, kicking out of her shoes.

Gretchen picked up the bridal bouquet that was waiting in a vase on the side table. She handed it over to Natalie with a touch of glassy tears in her eyes. "I can't believe this is happening. I'm so happy for you and Colin."

Natalie took a deep breath and nodded. "I can't believe it either, really. But let's make it happen before reality sets in and I launch into a panic attack. Go tell everyone the bride is ready and cue the musicians."

Gretchen disappeared and Natalie waited a few moments until she knew the doors to the chapel were closed. She stepped out to find her father, looking dumbfounded, on the bench outside. "Hi, Daddy."

He shot up from his seat, freezing as he saw her in her dress. "You look amazing. I'm not sure what's going on, but you look more beautiful than any bride I've ever seen in my life."

Natalie leaned in to hug him. "It's a long story, but I'm glad you're here."

The music grew louder, cueing up the bride. Natalie nearly reached for her headset before she remembered she was the bride this time. "Let's go get married, Daddy."

They walked to the doors and waited for them to swing open. The chapel was filled with people, all of them standing at the bride's arrival. It was hard for her to focus on any of them, though. Her eyes instantly went to the front of the chapel.

Colin stood there in his tuxedo, looking as handsome as ever. There wasn't a touch of nervousness on his face as he watched her walk down the aisle. There was nothing but adoration and love on his face. Looking into his eyes, she felt her own anxiety slip away. It was just like at the rehearsal. Everything faded away but the two of them.

Before she knew it, they'd walked the long aisle and were standing at the front of the chapel. Her father gave her a hug and a kiss on the cheek before passing her hand off to the waiting Colin. "Take care of my girl," he warned his future son-in-law before taking his seat.

They stepped up onto the raised platform together and waited for the pastor to start the ceremony.

"Dearly beloved, we gather here today to celebrate the blessed union of Frank and Lily."

Colin cleared his throat, interrupting the pastor as a rumble of voices traveled through the chapel. "Colin and Natalie," he corrected in a whisper.

The pastor's eyes widened in panic when he realized his mistake. Natalie had worked with this pastor before and knew that he had the names typed into his text. "Oh yes, so sorry. To celebrate the blessed union of *Colin and Natalie*."

The pastor continued on, but all Natalie could hear was the beating of her own heart. All she could feel was Colin's warm hand enveloping hers. When the pastor prompted them to turn and face each other, they did, and Natalie felt a sense of peace in Colin's gaze. He smiled at her, brushing his thumbs across the backs of her hands in a soothing motion.

"Are you okay?" he whispered.

Natalie nodded. She had never been better.

"Do you, Colin Edward Russell, take Natalie Lynn Sharpe to be your lawfully wedded wife? Will you love and respect her? Will you be honest with her? Will you stand by her through whatever may come until your days on this Earth come to an end?"

"I will."

"And do you, Natalie Lynn Sharpe, take Colin Edward Russell to be your lawfully wedded husband? Will you love and respect him? Will you be honest with him? Will you stand by him through whatever may come until your days on this Earth come to an end?"

She took a deep breath, a momentary flash of panic lighting in Colin's eyes. "I will," she said with a grin.

"Fra-*Colin*," the pastor stuttered. "What token do you give of the vows you have made?"

"A ring," Colin replied, pulling the same ring box from his coat pocket that he'd presented her with on the stage Wednesday night.

"You had the ring with you?" Natalie whispered.

"I was mad, but I hadn't given up on you yet." Colin opened the box and settled the exquisite diamond ring over the tip of her finger.

"Repeat after me. I give you this ring as a token of my vow." He paused, allowing Colin to respond. "With all that I am and all that I have, I honor you, and with this ring, I thee wed."

"...and with this ring, I thee wed," Colin repeated, slipping the ring onto her finger and squeezing her hand reassuringly.

"Natalie," the pastor asked, "what token do you give of the vows you have made?"

In an instant, Natalie's blood ran cold. She'd planned every moment, every aspect of this wedding. Everything but the rings. She had no ring. "I don't have anything," she whispered to the pastor.

The pastor hesitated, looking around the room for an answer to the problem as though there would be rings dangling from the ceiling on threads. This was probably the most stressful ceremony he'd ever done.

Even though she was the bride, Natalie was still a problem solver. She turned to the pews and the faces looking up at them. "Does anyone have a man's ring we can borrow for the ceremony?"

"I have a ring," a man said, getting up from Frankie's side of the chapel.

He was obviously a friend of Frankie's. They both shared a common love of bushy beards, tattoos and bow ties with matching suspenders. He jogged up the aisle, slipping a ring off his finger and handing it to Natalie.

"Thank you," she said. "We'll give it back as soon as we get a replacement."

"That's okay, you can keep it."

He returned to his seat and Natalie looked down at the ring in her hand. It was a heavy silver band with a skull centered on it. There were glittering red stones in the eye sockets. Natalie bit her lip to keep from laughing. A ring was a ring and that was what she needed. There was no being picky right now. She placed it on the tip of Colin's finger and repeated after the pastor.

It wasn't until the ring was firmly seated on his finger that Colin looked down. He snorted in a short burst of laughter and shook his head. Skulls must not be his thing.

The pastor didn't notice. He was probably just happy

they had rings and it was time to wrap up the ceremony. "Colin and Natalie, as you have both affirmed your love for each other and have made a promise to each other to live in this union, I challenge you both to remember to cherish each other, to respect each other's thoughts and ideas, and most important, to forgive each other. May you live each day in love, always being there to give love, comfort and refuge in the good times and the bad.

"As Colin and Natalie have now exchanged vows and rings, and pledged their love and faith for each other, it is my pleasure and honor to pronounce them Man and Wife. You may kiss the bride."

"This is the part I've been waiting for," Colin said with a wide smile. He took a step forward, cradling her cheeks in his hands and lifting her lips to his own.

"Wait," Natalie whispered just before their lips touched. "I need to tell you something."

Colin hesitated, his eyes wide with panic. She realized then that he thought she was changing her mind. "You won," she said quickly.

"Won what?" he asked.

"You won the bet," she admitted with a smile. "Merry Christmas, Mr. Russell. It's time to claim your prize."

"That I will. Merry Christmas, Mrs. Russell."

The kiss was soft and tender, holding the promise of a lifetime together and a thousand more kisses to come. It sent a thrill through her whole body, both from his touch and from the knowledge that they were now husband and wife. He had promised her a life-changing kiss and that's what he had delivered in more ways than one.

"I love you," he whispered as he pulled away, careful not to smear her lipstick before they took pictures.

She could barely hear him over the applause of the

crowd, but she would know the sound of those words coming from his lips anywhere. "I love you," she said.

"Please turn and face your family and friends," the pastor said, and they complied. "I am pleased to present for the first time, Mr. and Mrs. Colin Russell."

They stepped down the stairs together as man and wife while the crowd cheered. Hand in hand, they went down the aisle as their guests showered them with tiny bits of glittery white-and-silver confetti that looked like snow falling down on them.

They stepped through the doorway into the lobby. Waiting for them was Gretchen. She had picked up Natalie's headset, stepping in as wedding planner. "Congratulations." She held out a tray of champagne to them both and escorted them to the bridal suite to wait while the guests moved to the reception hall.

Alone in the suite, Colin wrapped one arm around her waist and pulled her tight against him. "You're all mine now," he growled into her ear.

"And you're all mine. For this Christmas and every one to follow."

Epilogue

One year later, Christmas Eve

Natalie slowly made her way through the renovated kitchen carrying the glazed Christmas ham. She intended to put it on the dining room table, but Colin was quick to intercept her and snatch the platter from her hands.

"What are you doing? You don't need to be carrying heavy things."

Natalie sighed and planted her hands on her hips. Being seven months pregnant was certainly a bigger challenge than she'd expected it to be, but she was making do. "I'm just pregnant. I'm perfectly capable of doing a lot of things."

Colin put the plate on the table and turned around. "I know you are. You're capable of amazing things, my wife." He kissed her on the lips. "I'd just much rather you enjoy yourself and your friends instead of being in the kitchen."

"Okay," she agreed, "but you come with me. All the food is out and we're ready to eat."

Hand in hand, they walked into the great room in what had once been the childhood home of Lily and Colin. When Frankie and Lily had returned from Vegas, Colin had still wanted to give them the house despite everything, but Lily hadn't wanted it. Just like the wedding, she was happy with the simple apartment and less hassle.

Instead, after they got married, Colin and Natalie took up residence there. She was all too happy to call the old house her home. He sold the supermodern mansion and she sold her townhouse. After a few renovations to update some things to their liking, they moved into the house. It was where she'd had her happiest childhood memories and once she found out she was pregnant, she wanted her child to have those kinds of memories in this home, too.

The rest of the From This Moment business partners and their spouses were loitering around the seating area, warming themselves by the fireplace. Newlyweds Bree and Ian were snuggling on the couch with glasses of wine. They'd finally tied the knot in October—oddly enough, the first of the group to get engaged and the last to wed.

Gretchen was feeding a chocolate *petit four* to Julian as they stood at the front window admiring the extensive Christmas lights display Colin had put together outside. They had married in the spring in a small chapel in Tuscany, fulfilling Gretchen's dream of seeing Italy at last.

"The food is ready," Natalie announced from the entryway.

Amelia was the first to get up from her seat by the fire. "I wish you would've let me help you with that. There's no need for you to manage the whole dinner by yourself. I know what it's like to cook at seven months pregnant."

"I'm fine. You're always doing the cooking. I wanted to do it. Besides, you've got baby Hope to worry about."

Amelia gestured over her shoulder to her husband Tyler. He was standing by the Christmas tree, letting their six-month-old look at the lights and shiny ornaments. "Not really. He's hardly put her down since the day she was born."

"Still. I'm fine. I might be out of practice when it comes to Christmas, but I can still manage cooking dinner."

"Okay, but we're doing the dishes," Amelia argued.

"Absolutely," Gretchen chimed in. "You're not lifting a single fork."

"I won't fight you on that. I hate doing the dishes."

The crowd all migrated into the dining room in a chaotic rumble of conversation and laughter. They took their places around the table, with Tyler slipping Hope into her high chair.

It was hard for Natalie to believe how much their lives had all changed in the past two years. They had all found amazing men and fallen madly in love. Each of them had married, and soon, there would be two babies playing in the new chapel nursery. It was enough to make her start tearing up at the dinner table.

Damn hormones.

"I'd like to thank everyone for joining us tonight for Christmas Eve dinner. The holidays are times to be spent with friends and family and I know how important all of you are to Natalie, and to me." Colin raised his glass to the group. "Merry Christmas, everyone."

The four couples sitting around the table each raised their glasses to toast a festive holiday season. "Merry Christmas," they all cheered.

* * * * *

Pick up these other BRIDES AND BELLES *stories from Andrea Laurence:*

Wedding planning is their business...
and their pleasure.

SNOWED IN WITH HER EX
THIRTY DAYS TO WIN HIS WIFE
ONE WEEK WITH THE BEST MAN

Available now! Only from Harlequin Desire.

If you're on Twitter, tell us what you think of Harlequin Desire! #harlequindesire

COMING NEXT MONTH FROM

Available January 5, 2016

#2419 TWIN HEIRS TO HIS THRONE

Billionaires and Babies • by Olivia Gates

Prince Voronov disappeared after he broke Kassandra's heart, leaving her pregnant and alone. Now the future king has returned to claim his twin heirs. Will he reclaim Kassandra's heart as part of the bargain?

#2420 NANNY MAKES THREE

Texas Cattleman's Club: Lies and Lullabies

by Cat Schield

Hadley Stratton is more than the nanny Liam Ward hired for his unexpected newborn niece. She's also the girl who got away...and the rich rancher is not going to let that happen twice!

#2421 A BABY FOR THE BOSS

Pregnant by the Boss • by Maureen Child

Is his one-time fling and current employee guilty of corporate espionage? Billionaire boss Mike Ryan believes so, but he'll need to reevaluate everything when he learns she's carrying his child...

#2422 PREGNANT BY THE RIVAL CEO

by Karen Booth

Anna Langford wants the deal—even though it means working with the guy she's never forgotten. But what starts as business turns into romance—until Anna learns of Jacob's ruthless motives and her unplanned pregnancy!

#2423 THAT NIGHT WITH THE RICH RANCHER

Lone Star Legends • by Sara Orwig

Tony can't believe the vision in red who won him at the bachelor auction. One night with Lindsay—his stubborn next-door neighbor—is all he'd signed up for. But her makeover has him forgetting all about their family feud!

#2424 TRAPPED WITH THE TYCOON

Mafia Moguls • by Jules Bennett

All that stands between mafia boss Braden O'Shea and what he wants is employee Zara Perkins. But when they're snowed in together, seduction becomes his only goal. Will he choose his family...or the woman he can't resist?

YOU CAN FIND MORE INFORMATION ON UPCOMING HARLEQUIN® TITLES, FREE EXCERPTS AND MORE AT WWW.HARLEQUIN.COM.

HDCNM1215

REQUEST YOUR FREE BOOKS!

2 FREE NOVELS PLUS 2 FREE GIFTS!

HARLEQUIN®

Desire

ALWAYS POWERFUL, PASSIONATE AND PROVOCATIVE

YES! Please send me 2 FREE Harlequin® Desire novels and my 2 FREE gifts (gifts are worth about $10). After receiving them, if I don't wish to receive any more books, I can return the shipping statement marked "cancel." If I don't cancel, I will receive 6 brand-new novels every month and be billed just $4.55 per book in the U.S. or $5.24 per book in Canada. That's a savings of at least 13% off the cover price! It's quite a bargain! Shipping and handling is just 50¢ per book in the U.S. and 75¢ per book in Canada.* I understand that accepting the 2 free books and gifts places me under no obligation to buy anything. I can always return a shipment and cancel at any time. Even if I never buy another book, the two free books and gifts are mine to keep forever.

225/326 HDN GH2P

Name (PLEASE PRINT)

Address Apt. #

City State/Prov. Zip/Postal Code

Signature (if under 18, a parent or guardian must sign)

Mail to the **Reader Service:**

IN U.S.A.: P.O. Box 1867, Buffalo, NY 14240-1867

IN CANADA: P.O. Box 609, Fort Erie, Ontario L2A 5X3

Want to try two free books from another line?
Call 1-800-873-8635 or visit www.ReaderService.com.

* Terms and prices subject to change without notice. Prices do not include applicable taxes. Sales tax applicable in N.Y. Canadian residents will be charged applicable taxes. Offer not valid in Quebec. This offer is limited to one order per household. Not valid for current subscribers to Harlequin Desire books. All orders subject to credit approval. Credit or debit balances in a customer's account(s) may be offset by any other outstanding balance owed by or to the customer. Please allow 4 to 6 weeks for delivery. Offer available while quantities last.

Your Privacy—The Reader Service is committed to protecting your privacy. Our Privacy Policy is available online at www.ReaderService.com or upon request from the Reader Service.

We make a portion of our mailing list available to reputable third parties that offer products we believe may interest you. If you prefer that we not exchange your name with third parties, or if you wish to clarify or modify your communication preferences, please visit us at www.ReaderService.com/consumerschoice or write to us at Reader Service Preference Service, P.O. Box 9062, Buffalo, NY 14240-9062. Include your complete name and address.

HD15

SPECIAL EXCERPT FROM

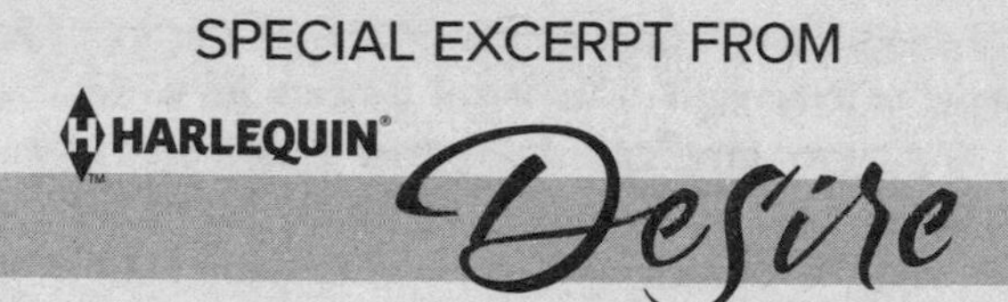

Prince Voronov disappeared after he broke Kassandra's heart, leaving her pregnant and alone. Now the future king has returned to claim his twin heirs. Will he reclaim Kassandra's heart, as well?

Read on for a sneak peek of
TWIN HEIRS TO HIS THRONE,
the latest in Olivia Gates*'s*
***BILLIONAIRES OF BLACK CASTLES** series.*

Kassandra fumbled for the remote, pushing every button before she managed to turn off the TV.

But it was too late. She'd seen him. For the first time since she'd walked out of his hospital room twenty-six months ago. That had been the last time the world had seen him, too. He'd dropped off the radar completely ever since. Now her retinas burned with the image of Leonid striding out of his imposing Fifth Avenue headquarters.

The man she'd known had been crackling with vitality, a smile of whimsy and assurance always hovering on his lips and sparkling in the depths of his eyes. This man was totally detached, as if he was no longer part of the world. Or as if it was beneath his notice. And there'd been another change. The stalking swagger was gone. In its place was a deliberate, almost menacing prowl.

This wasn't the man she'd known.

Or rather, the man she'd thought she'd known.

She'd long ago faced the fact that she'd known nothing of him. Not before she'd been with him, or while they'd been together, or after he'd shoved her away and vanished.

Kassandra had withdrawn from the world, too. She'd been pathetic enough to be literally sick with worry about him, to pine for him until she'd wasted away. Until she'd almost miscarried. That scare had finally jolted her to the one reality she'd been certain of. That she'd wanted that baby with everything in her and would never risk losing it. That day at the doctor's, she'd found out she wasn't carrying one baby, but two.

She'd reclaimed herself and her stability, had become even more successful career-wise, but most important, she'd become a mother to two perfect daughters. Eva and Zoya. She'd given them both names meaning life, as they'd given *her* new life.

Then Zorya had suddenly filled the news with a declaration of its intention to reinstate the monarchy. With every rapid development, foreboding had filled her. Even when she'd had no reason to think it would make Leonid resurface.

The doorbell rang.

It had become a ritual for her neighbor to come by and have a cup of tea so they could unwind together after their hectic days.

Rushing to the door, she opened it with a ready smile. "We should…"

Air clogged her lungs. All her nerves fired, short-circuiting her every muscle, especially her heart.

Leonid.

Right there. On her doorstep.

Don't miss TWIN HEIRS TO HS THRONE
by USA TODAY *bestselling author Olivia Gates,*
available January 2016 wherever
Harlequin® Desire books and ebooks are sold.

www.Harlequin.com

Copyright © 2016 by Olivia Gates

HDEXP1215

Turn your love of reading into rewards you'll love with

Harlequin My Rewards

Join for FREE today at www.HarlequinMyRewards.com

Earn **FREE BOOKS** of your choice.

Experience **EXCLUSIVE OFFERS** and contests.

Enjoy **BOOK RECOMMENDATIONS** selected just for you.

PLUS! Sign up now and get **500** points right away!

Earn FREE REWARDS Join Today! HarlequinMyRewards.com

MYRI6R

Love the Harlequin book you just read?

Your opinion matters.

Review this book on your favorite book site, review site, blog or your own social media properties and share your opinion with other readers!

Be sure to connect with us at:
Harlequin.com/Newsletters
Facebook.com/HarlequinBooks
Twitter.com/HarlequinBooks

HREVIEWS

JUST CAN'T GET ENOUGH?

Join our social communities
and talk to us online.

You will have access to the latest news on upcoming titles and special promotions, but most importantly, you can talk to other fans about your favorite Harlequin reads.

Harlequin.com/Community

Facebook.com/HarlequinBooks

Twitter.com/HarlequinBooks

Pinterest.com/HarlequinBooks

HSOCIAL

THE WORLD IS BETTER WITH *Romance*

Harlequin has everything from contemporary, passionate and heartwarming to suspenseful and inspirational stories.

Whatever your mood, we have a romance just for you!

Connect with us to find your next great read, special offers and more.

/HarlequinBooks

@HarlequinBooks

www.HarlequinBlog.com

www.Harlequin.com/Newsletters

HARLEQUIN®

A *Romance* FOR EVERY MOOD™

www.Harlequin.com

SERIESHALOAD2015